Unholy

By K.S. Garner

Published by K.S. Garner

Copyright © 2016 by K.S. Garner

Cover Design by: Rebecca Frank

Thank you for your
support, Rashad!
   -K.S. G—

D1521158

Unholy
License Notes

Dedication

Dedicated to my parents, the two people who believed in me before I had anything to believe in. They are the most genuine, supportive, and loving parents who have allowed me to be myself and to chase after my dreams. I can never truly repay you for everything but I hope they know my heart.

Chapter 1

"So who exactly did I allegedly kill this time?" I made my voice as cocky as possible to hide my growing fear.

The interrogation room they used crawled in on me with creepy steps. It looked like it might have been an old storage room at one point. Old shelves lined one wall, and faded signs curled at the edges. Overhead, the dim bulb flickered, revealing abandoned file boxes cluttered in the corner by the door. If this was a desperate attempt to intimidate me during questioning, I hated to admit it was working. A little. The size of the space combined with the stench of stale food and musty papers caused my stomach to tighten. My fear of closed in spaces reared its ugly head.

"Is that all you have to say?" The detective's voice reeked of fatigue. Onion-sized pit stains marred his blue, retail-store button-down and creases lined his worn khakis in a zig-zag pattern. Cop clothes.

"Yep." I ducked my head to hide my true concern. I'd been here for hours according to the football shaped clock on the wall and saw no end in sight. I sighed and threw my head back, staring at the brown water stains on the faded ceiling tiles. This was beyond ridiculous. My wrists ached, but so far no one had the decency to remove my handcuffs.

They never read me my rights, so I couldn't actually be charged with anything, right? I shifted in my chair and tried to ease the growing numbness in my butt. Way to keep a girl uncomfortable.

"Is that how you want to play it?" Detective Long asked with a harsh exhalation.

He had to be as exhausted as me at this point. Tiny lines fanned out from his brown eyes and the corners of his mouth pinched tight. He couldn't figure out how to connect me with the guy at the bus stop. I wasn't helping either.

"Yep," I repeated with emphasis on the 'p'.

Sighing, the detective roughly pushed his chair back and left the room without another word, leaving me alone. *Again.* He wanted me to stew and think he had something on me. This was his third time abandoning me to my anxiety. Normally the room alone would do the job, but in light of the circumstances I was already on edge. This wasn't my first go-round with law enforcement and unfortunately with my history, I highly doubted it would be my last.

I leaned back in the chair on two legs, trying without success to get comfortable and closed my eyes. They'd probably hold me overnight since the desk officer had confiscated my ID and cash. Her dark glare had silently confirmed there was no way in hell I was getting out of here anytime soon.

I tried to rehash everything that happened at the bus stop. The guy had tried to snatch my purse. I'd gripped his wrist when he attempted to rush pass me. Next thing I know, he was seizing all over the ground. Not that it hadn't happened before around me.

Of course the good citizens of Baltimore had flagged down a passing cop who showed before I could disappear. Next thing I know, they needed to take me in for questioning. I bit my lip. The only thing they could really stick me with was being in the wrong place at the wrong time and last time I checked that wasn't a crime.

The shadows on the wall lengthened and my breath caught.[1]

In your nose and out your mouth. In your nose and out your mouth. I repeated my private mantra to settle my anxiety until my fear eased.

I wasn't sure how long I'd been chanting to myself when the door opened again. I didn't bother to look up at whoever entered the room. I wasn't in the mood for another round of questions otherwise known as let's see if she'll crack.

"Misti Calloway, what a pleasure to finally meet you."

The greeting had me slamming the chair down on all four legs. The sounds of shoes clacking on the tiled floor drew close to me. Icy fingers ran across my knuckles and I immediately reeled back from the stranger.

"Now, now, my dear, calm down."

I turned to face a woman jingling a pair of keys as she spoke. I remained still, holding my wrists close to my chest as I stared. She wore a dark navy blue striped suit with a crisp white shirt buttoned to the collar. Not cop clothes. Too high end for that. Lawyer, maybe?

Shadows fell, blocking the dim lighting. A cloud of darkness cloaked the room, almost suffocating me. I focused on the cold and slim fingers. The idea of them grazing my skin again sent a wave of goose bumps over my body.

"Misti, fear not, for I am here to help, dear."

I lowered my arms onto the scarred, wooden table. I hadn't even realized my arms were above my head with my face buried in the inside of my elbows, hidden away from the mysterious person.

She replaced the detective and sat in the chair across the table from me. Her pale hands were now folded over one another, face devoid of any emotion.

After a moment, she slowly reached over to my wrists and unlocked the handcuffs. This time I tried not to jerk away from the cold touch.

"Finally!" I sighed in relief as I rubbed my irritated skin.

However, all color drained from my face by what I saw next. I didn't know whether to make heads or tails of what I saw next. Her jaw elongated. High cheek bones cut through a rounded face. Dark almond-shaped eyes and a smooth forehead that lacked eyebrows shifted into a gruesome image. In less than a split second the features morphed back, leaving me to wonder if my imagination was playing a new trick.

The lighting in here was piss-poor to say the least. The bridge of her nose was long and slim, and the nostril was sharp at the tip. Long and thick blonde hair tumbled down her back. Nothing monstrous.

"Who are you?"

Nothing. She continued to watch me with a hint of a smile.

Maybe she knew something I didn't.

"Do you know what happened to that guy?"

Again, nothing.

For a moment, despair got the better of me. "At least tell me if that dude is dead or not. Please!"

Unholy

One minute I stood beside a young guy on the bus stop and he reached for my purse strap. The next my hand touched his chest and his eyes bulged, mouth gaping, right before he fell over on the ground. Screams and chaos ensued as the other commuters gathered around us.

When the police arrived, I was sent on a one-way ride here with no idea what had happened. Well, I kinda knew since something similar had happened to me before. My personal count on dropping bodies was up to seven.

"Oh, he's definitely dead. But don't worry. He was just another being who didn't appreciate his second chance and is now back where he belongs."

"Why, me?" I begged aloud. "Why do I get stuck with the wackos?"

It had been a long day and I was too tired for any of this shit. "Look, am I being charged with something or am I free to go? I don't have time for any of your foolishness . . . whoever you are."

"Is it not exquisite . . . astounding, really? How everything can change in an instant, life as we know it, whether for better or worse? Even our second chances never pan out the way we hope."

I rolled my eyes. More crack pot mumbo-jumbo. "Look, I'm not sure what your gig is. I'm out as soon as they realize they got nothin' on me. I didn't do anything to that guy. He tried to grab my purse but then he died. I mean, I shoved him and all but not hard."

I'd practiced that lie during the whole ride down to the station. Not getting a response, I threw my head on my arms onto the table. Melodrama was my go-to when

I got scared. My head throbbed, the signs of a nice migraine to go with the rest of this cluster.

"The man is no longer alive. He never was. However, thanks to you, my dear, my decade-long search has finally ended."

No idea what that meant. It didn't sound good for me, so I didn't bother to lift my head. Being one of those drama queens I aspired to felt really good right about now.

"You have a great talent," she continued. "One that would be a shame to go to waste."

As she spoke, I became aware of her movements around the table. Suddenly, her voice spoke directly in my ear. I didn't bother to lift my head. I could feel the burn of her stare digging holes into my skull.

"Allow me to offer you an opportunity to control yourself, my dear Misti. To give you a fair chance to prove yourself. To hone your great skills and talents a book could never teach you."

I tilted my head only enough to see the determined gaze through my narrowed eyes. We stared at one another for a few moments as I chewed my bottom lip.

"Who are you?" I finally asked.

A grin slowly crept onto that soft, angular face as she rose again.

"The man with a plan, my dear Misti. And more importantly, the man who's going to get you the hell out of here and give you a real chance at life."

Huh. He was a man after all.

Chapter 2

I don't need this in my life! I just wanna go home!

I would have said that out loud if I wasn't such a chicken shit. I really wanted to dodge the lean figure and race for freedom out the door. Instead, I stuck with, "Huh?"

Then, my mystery guest casually strolled back around the other side of the table and to the door. He came to a halt, one hand reaching for the handle.

"They won't let you go, you know. The evidence is thin at best but he was alive until you touched him. Witnesses will attest to that. Police don't like mysterious deaths. They'll keep you until something sticks."

I jumped to my feet, his words causing my heart to race. "Who are you? Are you my cheap ass appointed attorney? You can't be because you really suck at this 'talk and we'll give you a deal' speech."

He just laughed. Without another word, he opened the door and left.

In through your nose. Out your mouth. In and out. In and out.

I cursed under my breath but that didn't stop me from creeping toward the door, inch by inch, until I could peek over the threshold. And . . . no one. The office was completely empty as if they all forgot about little old me stewing in their back dinky interrogation room.

They wouldn't just let me leave, would they? There's no way. I gained courage with each foot forward through the office until I reached the exit. I stopped and took one last look around. What are the odds the place would be cleared out when I sought to disappear? I waited for an officer to pop out and haul me to a crowded cell.

No one jumped out from the corners. No one screamed for me to stop. Despite the alarms going off in my head, I hauled tail through the corridor and out the main entrance. I emerged through the doors and searched the unusually quiet street for a way to get back home.

"Wise choice, Misti."

"Shit!" I jumped, a hand to my pounding chest.

The stranger chuckled and handed me something. The hand was turned palm down so I couldn't see what it held, but I extended my hand anyway.

My ID and cash.

"Any longer and I would have become worried you weren't who I perceived you to be. Come, we must be on our way."

He turned toward a big ass black truck parked at the curb, but I didn't follow.

"I'm not going anywhere with you," I called from the cracked sidewalk as the distance between us grew.

He stopped and stared at me, those eerie dark eyes unblinking.

"I have no idea who you are or what you're about. I appreciate you helping me out, but I can't go with you." I gestured toward my stuff he gave back. "Thank you."

With that I was on my way. I didn't hear any footsteps or tire tracks follow me, and I turned to make sure. Our eyes met as we stared at each other once more. Then, he got in the backseat and drove off.

"And may I never see you again, you strange man, you.

Chapter 3

I knew downtown pretty well and still got turned around a few times, catching one bus then the subway. I recognized more than a few of the brick row homes I normally passed on the public transit and eventually made it to my apartment the rest of the way on foot.

"Home, sweet home." I climbed the narrow staircase, careful of the loose step half-way up. I fiddled with the lock a few times before the tumbler finally clicked. The strong, familiar smell of bologna and sickening dust greeted me. I made a bee-line for the bed shoved against a corner wall and crawled onto it. Falling face first sounded like a great idea, but falling on this bed felt like face planting on a stack of bricks.

Well, it wasn't a bed as much as a mattress on top of a long crate my landlord planned to throw out. Luckily enough I caught the garbage men before they dumped it. I timed it just right to make my grab and now got to sleep a few inches off the floor at night.

My makeshift kitchen behind the adjacent wall contained a column-sized stove, oven, and sink as one package. My landlord also provided me with a mini-refrigerator when I rented the apartment. And just my luck, it was at least ten years old. The inside never lit up no matter how many times I added a new light bulb, and contained these frighteningly unknown stains I refused to allow to touch any food I put in there.

The bathroom matched the size of a coat closet. Every day I had to be careful not to hit my legs on the sink when I got out of the shower. And thankfully the shower was one of those stand alone deals because a tub wouldn't fit. The apartment rested above a deli so the distinct stench of moldy cheese was one I'd grown accustomed to.

The constant chill due to the wheezing furnace kept the whole place breezy and forced me to stay clothed no matter what time of the day it was. I shouldn't complain. The place was cheap and the owner was looking to rent it out to make some extra cash.

It was a decision made out of desperation. Sometimes my rash ideas paid off, sometimes not so much. My stomach erupted in a familiar growl. I settled for a glass of tepid water and a stale bag of mini cookies filched from my landlord's restaurant below.

Nibbling on an oatmeal cookie, I ventured over to the window and squinted over the dark and empty street. The distinct rumble of the subway and distant sirens broke through the night. I was lamenting my fate as a product of the urban streets of Baltimore when the power went out. I waited a few seconds to see if the generator would kick it back on.

Still nothing. Not even the muted hum of my fridge. I could make out the lights from an apartment across the street before they blinked off, and then the street lamps was suddenly doused too. One by one the area darkened. I choked on a cookie crumble and the hair at the back of my neck curled.

The silence was enough to worry me. No panicked screams or cries of distress rang out. I'm not sure if this happened often. Normally by this time I'm working my overnight shift at the morgue. Ironically enough, I didn't have to work tonight.

"Nothing to get worked up about." I headed for my bed and stretched out on my uncomfortable mattress.

Click, click, click.

Washa, washa, washa. I pried one eye open at the soft noises by the door.

Cack, cack, cack.

Definitely getting louder now. I threw the blanket off my legs and tip-toed across the floor, feet curling against the cold hardwood.

I took karate classes as a kid. I can fight. How hard can this be? One punch after the other at the guy's face. No different than a school yard brawl. Just hope he wasn't taller than 5'4" and I'd be good. Maybe.

Shit, who was I kidding? My stomach rolled at the thought. Calling the cops should have been my first thought if I was any other person and this was any other day. Instead, I hid in a tiny bathroom waiting for my soon-to-be-intruder wearing sweatpants, a tank top, and carrying an old ice pick from beneath my pillow.

Finally, the intruder got through my flimsy locks and bulldozed through the door. Without noticing where I stood in shadows, he began loudly rummaging through anything with a handle. Typical, I'd get a bumbling idiot for my first break and enter.

He didn't bother with a disguise. Apparently, plain, dirty street clothes would suffice for tonight's misdeeds. I prayed he wouldn't find my savings stash. Money I'd duct taped under the sink. If there was any God or deity looking out for me tonight now would be the night to earn their keep with me.

No dice.

Unholy

He yanked open one of the kitchen drawers and randomly grabbed what he could. Mainly cheap jewelry I didn't care about then he discovered my wad as he scrounged some more. Soon after, his sneakers scratched along the floor as he headed my way. Although he could take the cheap jewelry, he couldn't have the money. It was all I had to get by on until my next check. Before he could yank the narrow door open, I lunged for him.

We both screamed and scrambled for a few seconds. When he broke free, I fell backward. He pushed me hard before fleeing down the narrow stairway.

I heard him stumble a bit on his way down. I hurried after him, only thinking of my money. I hopped the last four steps and onto the guy's back as he reached the bottom. The jump threw us both onto Mr. Liam's shop floor, but I was back on my feet quicker than him. He lunged in my direction, and we struggled once again.

The punches to my side stung but I bit back the cry of pain and wrestled for the strap of his pack. As soon as his arm reared back, I seized my moment and slammed my palm to his mid-section. My fingers began a familiar tingle. He dropped to all fours, looking at me in a new light. He jerked, face morphing into huge jowls with deep, pulsing veins, red eyes and fangs sprouted from his mouth.

"Holy…!" I pushed away, scrambling backward.

He pushed up onto his knees and looked at me, eyes glaring. "Who are you?"

The voice wasn't what I expected. Suddenly the tones were deeper and with a gravelly pitch. Before I could think of an answer his body slumped over and his head hit the ground with a thud. Horror crept up my body, prickling my arms as the hairs stood up.

It wasn't enough that I worked around death and smelled its remnants on my skin on a daily basis. Now I'd done it again. One more notch for the freaky stuff that had been happening to me since I was twelve.

I remained on the cold floor, palms flat in shock. Tears blinded my vision as I crawled over to him to check for a pulse, stopping a few times for a hiccup. I looked up at the bright moon shining through the window. I stared for a while then back to the man. His features were normal again, his mouth hung slightly open, and his eyes were empty.

I rose from the floor and started for the stairs. What I really wanted to do was holler to the high heavens.

Then, I glanced around and wondered what to do next. Should I hide his body? This wasn't going to look good for me.

Grabbing the body by the old school tennis, I dragged him to the door. Slowly, I peered over the threshold for any nosy neighbors and came face to face with a shiny silver shield.

Chapter 4

For the second time that evening, I was about to be interviewed by the police. An officer shoved me into the back of a squad car. This one smelled like vomit and even had traces of it on the floor. I wasn't in handcuffs at least, but I knew that could change in a matter of seconds. In fact, I saw silver bracelets in my future once they connected me to the bus stop guy. My good old buddy Detective Dennis Long would not be pleased.

Once the cops questioned me and recognized my name from my last visit to the station, I was in trouble. Getting dead seemed to happen a lot around me. And this last guy…something *did* happen with his face. Demon-like features were not normal.

My eyes started to well but I furiously blinked them away. I threw my head back against the headrest and closed my eyes. *What the hell was going on?*

The meaningless chit chat of the officers and murmurs of spectators surrounding the scene soon faded. A dark shadow appeared over the back window behind my eyelids. Shivers flowed over my arms again as I opened my eyes to a familiar sight. The strange man from the police station.

"Hello, Misti. We meet again." His smug greeting burned me.

"What do you want? I don't have time for your games."

"Come out, my dear, and let's properly introduce ourselves." He opened the car door as if it hadn't been locked moments ago and extended one of those clammy hands toward me. Hesitantly, I placed my hand in his, and he led me away from the cop car.

"Wait, where are we going?" I peered over my shoulder just as two men from the coroner's office loaded up the ominous black bag containing the intruder on the stretcher. It wasn't closed all the way. I couldn't see much but at least his mouth was closed this time and I assumed they'd closed his eyes as well.

"Should we be leaving like this? Won't they be looking for me, for us?" My questions didn't stop me from wandering right along. Freedom trumped doing the right thing any day.

The same black SUV from earlier whipped in front of us, coming to an abrupt halt at the curb. Without hesitation, my rescuer pulled the rear door open, hopped in and scooted aside while patting the seat cushion for me to get in.

"This is crazy, you know that right?" I risked a glance over my shoulder. No one looked our way so I dove in. "The police will put a warrant out for my arrest and think I'm guiltier than they already BELIEVE I am!"

For once he almost looked sincere. "Aaron had an unfortunate appetite for power. Raw energy was always his weakness. I didn't expect him to stoop to petty robbery once I let him loose though." His lips curled in a scary smile. "And of course he should have known better than to go against the likes of you."

"What do you mean?" My heart skipped a beat. Was he admitting that my burglar was something *more*?

"This, Misti," he pointed at the scene outside my apartment, "is no longer your concern. This is no longer your life. We must move toward the future, and that includes you, physically, mentally, and emotionally removed from your past."

Wow, more crack pot talk. I couldn't help staring. He'd changed clothes and wore a black button down, matching jacket and pants with yellow and pink patterned geometric shapes, like no shit, and a pair of black ankle boots rockers wore in the late seventies completing the image. No more lawyer suits. Dude, had to be tripping on some good stuff.

"You know what, I don't get half of what you're talking about and right now I don't care."

An explosion rocked the street around us causing me to jerk around and look out the window.

"Whoa!" Flames poured from the window upstairs to my apartment. Shards of glass all over the street and over the cowering crowd of spectators and officers. "Shit! Damn!"

My profanity was brought on by another explosion. This time the squad car, specifically the one I had been in, burst into a giant fireball and all the while, my riding partner laughed like a loon. My gaze snapped back to him in disbelief.

"Don't worry, no one was in it, dear," he assured me. Again, he reached his slim fingers toward me. "Allow me to introduce myself. Randall. Randall Clark, at your service."

Chapter 5

The car ride was made in silence but that didn't stop my mind from whirling at a hundred miles an hour. After several seemingly random turns we reached a brick building I immediately recognized. The Chief Medical Examiner's office.

I paled and turned to Randall. "We need to leave. I'm not supposed to be here after hours. If we get caught, we're definitely going to prison."

I hadn't actually done any real time, but I'd been in enough jails for questioning and knew I didn't want to extend any future stays there. The BCPD worked fast. As quickly as they found me with that dead guy at my place, they'd connect this break-in to me. I had a sudden vision of my face plastered up on the walls in every office across the DMV.

"We have one small task to accomplish here. A confirmation of what I already know, you could say."

"No to whatever that is."

His thin lips turned down in the face of my protest as if he tasted something nasty. The driver jumped out and opened the door for us. I knew this building front to back, inside and out. I didn't recall ever seeing Randall here, but he seemed to know his way as evidenced by the fact he waltzed right up to the front door.

"Randall, how did you—I mean…where are the night shift guards? Surely someone's bound to catch us." My heart beat an uneven rhythm in my chest.

"That's not meant for you to worry about." We stopped at a familiar pair of double doors. "I have other means for you to use that brains on, my dear." He entered the alarm code by the doors and then unlocked it.

If Randall entering the building like he owned it wasn't suspicious enough, the keys and security definitely was. I always had to be let in by a guard and they hovered over me like a hawk.

Immediately, Randall started for the lower rooms where freezer slabs were housed and playfully knocked on its metal doors.

I yanked at my hair. "Quit that! Have some respect."

He grinned, then pulled a small wheeled table over to the center of the room, in front of the metal doors. He placed three keys down on the table, and smiled at me. Man, did he need some serious work on his grill. The smile tugged at his cheeks so unnaturally tight his smooth skin looked on the verge of cracking. "Peek-a-boo, who is who?"

"Am I supposed to know what that means? What are we doing? What if someone hears us?" Then, a horrible thought hit me. "Did you bring me along to help you steal a body?!"

Seriously? As if my luck couldn't get any worse. This was taking crazy too far.

"One of these is not like the rest." He snickered and it wasn't a humorous sound.

"So I do what exactly? Spot the difference and we part ways. What's the catch, Randall?" There had to be one. Leave it to me to get mixed up in this insane mess. I chalked this up to number one on the list of jacked up crap happening to me lately. Dead bodies, power outages and now this no dressing fool.

He leaned in close and whispered, "My dear, you have a gift. A talent, I've been searching forever for." Randall, if that really was his name, smiled again. It was supposed to be reassuring but it just made me feel worse.

I didn't like the sound of that. No one knew about the disturbing things that would not be mentioned. I barely knew what the hell was wrong with me.

"I shall be back shortly, my dear." He straightened to his full height and pushed away from me. One more ghoulish smile then he left me alone with the bodies.

I sought out a wheeled stool and sat. *In and out.* I had no idea what to do. Figure out his half-ass riddle or head for the hills. After the fifth exhale, I stared at the first closed metal door. I choked and almost leaped from my seat.

My reflection showed my image. I no longer wore my sweatpants and tank top. Instead I had on blue scrubs and my battered tennis.

How the Hell?

A man barreled through the double doors.

"Shit." I jumped up, wondering if this was the point when everything fell apart.

We awkwardly stared at one another. He wore identical blue scrubs head to toe with a paper thin mask under his chin. His slightly bronzed skin paled at running into me. He rocked back on his heels, continuing to watch me with his big brown eyes and the longest eye lashes I'd ever seen on a man. The slight cant to his eyes and other features hinted at a Middle Eastern ancestry.

The silence grated so I blurted, "Um, I'm here for Mr. Randall Clark. He asked me to examine a body. You may have seen him down the hall."

The new guy frowned, his mouth falling open as his gaze searched the room. He stepped further inside looking for my accomplice no doubt.

"Maybe you can help." I eased toward the wheeled table as I babbled. "I'm just getting started."

"You're the one everyone won't shut up about." He braced his hands on his hips and smirked. It looked good on him.

"Everyone?" I asked. *More people know about us being here? About me?*

He swiped a hand over his head and rubbed at the back of his buzz cut. Eventually, he came closer, hand extended. "Wentz. Axel Wentz."

"Calloway. Misti Calloway." It seemed ridiculous considering, but we shook hands.

On the plus side, his hand was hot and solid like any other guy. There was no weird tingling, ju-ju vibrating through my fingers but I felt as if I'd met this man before. What made it even stranger was that he wasn't looking at me but at our hands. He maintained a strong grip and kept flexing his fingers around mine like he was hoping for a response.

It wasn't until I coughed deliberately that he let me go. We stood there awkwardly a bit before he spoke again. "So, uh, let's get started, Calloway."

No one called me by my last name but I went with it.

Axel walked toward the lone desk and moved things around. He returned to me with a notepad and clipboard. I took them not sure why I needed them.

"I don't mean to be rude, Wentz," I followed his lead. "How long have you known this Randall guy?"

He snorted. "Call me Axel."

I nodded as if this was totally normal and on the up and up. "Call me Misti."

"Maybe." His grin bordered on insolent but I let him get away with it. His presence was easing some of the bubbles in my stomach caused by Randall leaving me here with his mystery quest.

"Let's see if you have what it takes." Axel angled his dark, fuzzy head toward the drawers where the bodies were kept.

Unsure of where to start, I unlocked all three slab doors closest to me. "Randall only said one's not the same."

Axel's mouth firmed and he folded his arms over his chest.

"Fine," I huffed and yanked open the first drawer.

The man's chest was caved in. I opened the second and held in a gasp. I worked here, the condition of the bodies shouldn't bother me but sometimes they did. Life was precious and snatched away in a blink.

Bruises marred the old lady over her arms and legs. I jotted down a possibility of assault contrary to the "heart attack" listed on her tag. The last drawer held a younger woman who didn't have any visible injuries. Death listed as "unknown". I ignored my unease and checked her toes. The skin under the nail bed, including the nails was black and blue with signs of rot. After peeling her mouth and nostrils open, they only confirmed my theory—addict.

Living in Baltimore, I'd seen one too many addicts. I didn't understand the task Randall set before me. These people didn't need to be examined, their cause of death was obvious to any person after watching one episode of a late night drama show. I tossed the clipboard onto the small table and began pushing the bodies back inside their frozen crypts.

"Was that it? Did you get what Randall needed?" Axel asked, shoulder leaning against the pale walls as I went to wash my hands at a corner sink.

"I don't know what else to do." Something banged from inside. I jolted. "Do you hear that?"

"Huh?"

Another bang, this time louder.

"There it is again. You seriously don't hear that?" I turned off the water as we both cocked our heads to the side for the noise. This time wheezing echoed from one of the small metal slab doors. Careful not to interrupt the sudden noise, I halted next to the drawer I'd closed when it suddenly stopped.

Axel's brow creased and he eyed me as if I was the only looney in this play. "What do you—?"

"Shush!"

We remained silent for a bit. Seconds ticked by. The room lost its chill, a warm breeze skirting up my sweaty scrubs. I could tell by Axel's puzzled look that he didn't hear anything

I'm hearing things now. My own personal hell above ground.

I was afraid to face Axel in case he saw the worry I tried to hide. How many times in my childhood had strange things happened to me?

"I think I'm thirsty," I muttered, staring at the overhead ceiling lights.

The door to the room opened and shut behind us. The faucet turned on, water filled the sink then shut off abruptly.

BOOM, BOOM, BOOM.

"Please tell me you heard that?" I twisted back around to Axel, who had just as much shock on his face as mine. We stood still until we heard the banging again definitely coming from inside the drawer nearest my hip.

Thank goodness he heard it too. Maybe there was an end in sight to my brand of crazy.

I look towards Axel for direction but he wanted none of it. So much for chivalry. I tip-toed to the drawer between each frightening bang then suddenly the small door popped open. A creature slid out resembling a human sized tarantula.

"Holy shit, what is that?" Axel gasped.

"I don't know." I backed away, tripping over my feet. "That wasn't there when I opened the drawer, you were here."

"Well, kill it!" Axel said.

"What, no, you do it you're the man!" I yelled.

"Yeah, but Randall told you to figure out the problem not me."

I arched a brow in his direction and muttered, "Thanks."

27

Unholy

The spider like creature contorted its limbs to crawl on all fours, belly lowered to the floor. Its two sets of eyes followed Axel and I as we hovered in the corner. When its gaze landed on me large pinchers snapped in my direction. Frantically, I began to throw anything and everything I could at the creature from the shelves behind me.

Axel's eyes widened. "That's your great plan?"

Ignoring him, I continued my impression of a major league ball player. Go Baltimore!

The beast hopped along the floor doing its on impression of a school kid playing hopscotch to avoid my ineffective missiles.

"If that thing starts spitting anything other than webs from its butt, I'm going to be really pissed."

Just then, webs of acid spit out from the creature, but from the mouth, luckily. I glared at Axel in blame. "Really? Would you like to give it other ideas."

"Would you quit messing around and kill that damned thing?" He demanded as he tried to climb the wall behind us.

"I'm trying," I yelled back, wanting to laugh at the turn of events. Only me. "It's only some weird, demonic spider from my worse nightmare. Give me a minute."

Axel was no help and darted to the door when his attempts to scale the wall failed. After trying to pry them open which was a no go, we continued to dance around the spider creature, and throwing whatever wasn't bolted down at it.

"There's got to be something you can do," Axel huffed as we cowered behind the overturned table, the creature hissing and snapping at us. "I have an idea but you're not going to like it."

I canted my head in his direction. "That sounds vague. I already don't like it."

"Tough shit." Axel slid a hand towards the cabinet under the sink. He gathered an arm full of random chemicals, and started twisting the tops off.

"What are you doing?" I wasn't one to wait for a prince to save me or anything but dude seriously needed to step up his game and save the day.

I covered my mouth and nose when the smallest hint of the contents inside began seeping into the air. Then, I noticed the quiet and the curls at my nape tightened. I dared a peek over the table. Nothing. It was gone.

"Uh…Axel, where did that thing go?"

"What?" Focused on his task, he barely glanced up.

The large creature couldn't have gone far so I shouldn't have been shocked when it gave us a surprise attack, crawling along the ceiling right above us.

I screamed and pushed Axel in its path. "Every man for himself."

The thing began spewing acid down. Sizzling holes appeared in the floor. Axel grabbed his stupid bottles and fled across the room. He shot a dark look at me. "Give me a minute. I'm going to distract it and then you can send it back."

I looked at him as if he'd lost his mind and maybe he had. "Send it back? Let me put this in words even you can understand…hell to the no."

Unfortunately, the spider thing crawled down the wall and headed in my direction. It had me cornered and spat acid, nearly burning off the edge of my neon high tops. It inched closer, savoring every moment before its pinchers snapped on my bones and munched on my dead body.

Suddenly, the creature veered back from me with a loud screeching howl. Confused, I looked towards what scared it. Axel was spraying the chemicals onto the back of the beast.

"Now what?" I asked after running to get to his side.

He gave me an odd look, brows lowered. "Hit it! Touch it! You know, the thing you're supposed to do."

"What no, I'm not touching that thing!" That's how people died in horror movies.

"Do you want to get out of here or not? I'm running out of spray here." His squirt bottle held a dwindling amount of liquid.

Without giving me time to brace, Axel shoved me forward.

I couldn't believe it. I wanted to throat punch him but more important things faced me. I charged at the super spider and leaped on its furry back. Disgusting. I wailed on it. I threw my fists in every which way. I didn't care what I hit.

My hand tingled and burned. A dark patch appeared on the furred skin. The spider squirmed beneath me. I rolled to the floor and landed awkwardly. I couldn't take my eyes off the creature as it shriveled on itself and vanished.

"Is it over?" Groans from Axel broke my trance "Are you alright?"

I popped him on the top of his head with the palm of my hand. "No thanks to you, moron."

"Ah, not exactly how I thought you'd handle things."

Axel and I both spun at Randall's sudden reappearance, catching us off guard. I wondered if he'd been there longer with Axel and I too engrossed to notice.

"It has been a long night, and I'm sure you both are quite tired. Shall we leave, we have other business to attend to." Randall lightly steered me with a hand at my lower back. He led me outside of the facility and back to the SUV. "Come along, Mr. Wentz."

Baltimore was starting to feel a lot like Kansas, and I made a mental note to pick up some red shoes in case I needed a fast out from this upcoming whirlwind.

Chapter 6

It was still dark when our truck stopped in front of a large brick mansion. I'd recognized a couple of exits heading toward the county. High privacy hedges perfectly manicured surrounded the grounds. We were definitely not in the city. Randall unlocked the iron gate to let me through first. Three impressive levels rose up, plantation shutters added to the stately appeal, and a wraparound porch on the bottom level screamed old money. The kind you could smell a mile away.

An old swing bench creaked on the porch, worn cushions in a faded red showing long gone butt imprints. Beside the bench was a small side table with an ashtray on top. I didn't smell any lingering smoke, so it had to have been out here for a while.

I turned back towards the others following up the walkway.

Randall and Axel joined me on the porch but stopped short at the sight of the ashtray. Randall's lips firmed as he glared in the direction of the driver hidden from our view. I had a feeling he'd wait until we were all inside before he reemerged for his verbal lashing.

Randall led the way through the front door. I expected the interior to be as extravagant and orderly as the exterior. Not a time capsule frozen in the forties of an old Hollywood home. Creaky hardwood floors, dusty area carpets, paint chipping off the staircase, mail piled up covering the entire table by the door. Axel veered off to the left and disappeared through another door.

Randall nudged my shoulder, leaving me to go with him when I wished I could chase after Axel. With him I felt as if I had a co-conspirator. Randall, on the other hand, left me with the willies. Goosebumps crawled up my arms as I ended up in the sitting room.

At least the room didn't appear to hide any strange surprises. There was a chess table setup in the far left corner, the pieces moved about in play. In the center of the room sat a red, very comfy, and worn armchair angled in front of the fireplace. Area rugs dominated the space, placed only under the chairs and extending the length of the room.

I ignored Randall's smirk as he let me check out the new place. I knelt in front of the fireplace to get a closer look at the decorative motif. It portrayed a centaur hunting a nude woman and man through the forest. Scars covered the man's muscular body. The nude woman's mouth was parted in a scream as she attempted to flee the beast.

"I'm so pleased at how wonderful you're turning out to be," Randall interrupted. "I think you'll do very well for what I have planned."

"How about sharing the plan with the person involved?" My snark was on level ten.

"A battle is coming and I want you on my side.

"What the...? I'm not interested in any battles." I backed up, waving my hands. "And you know what else? I'm getting off this merry-go-round of horror."

I didn't think it possible but his eyes darkened more than before. I caught a glimpse of my distorted reflection in the bottomless orbs. His lips curled into a snarl. "You will do as I say, Misti Calloway."

"Yeah, that's a no." I flipped him the bird and headed for the door. "I'm done, dude. Nothing you can say can make me stay."

"If you walk out of that door, you'll never understand the gift and abilities you were born with," Randall warned.

"Fuuuuuck!" I stopped, hands braced on the door frame and dropped my head. "What do you know about me and cut the crap?"

With measured steps, I turned and faced him. Randall held up a hand and ticked off facts on his fingers. "You've always been different but never knew how. And most important people end up dead around you. If you want the truth, you'll stay and discover a whole new world. One where you fit right in."

"Is that why you rescued me from the police station, made them all disappear off to Neverland so I could check out undetected? And what about the bodies at the morgue? You never mentioned that…that thing." Then it hit me once again so hard, I finally faced Randall.

"You knew that creature was in there the whole time, didn't you?" I screwed up my face and imitated his voice. "One is not the same blah, blah."

He didn't bother answering. Only smiled and crossed his arms, snaking his delicate fingers through his elbows. "Do you want to know or not?"

My mind raced. Every since I was a little kid weird stuff happened to me. I'd seen a movie about a kid who saw dead people and told my mom I saw them too. Or something similar. The monsters I sometimes saw were the stuff of nightmares. Of course that didn't go over so well.

Neither did the tingling sensation in my hands when I touched someone or was even within a five-foot radius of something creepy. Did I complain? Nope. That wasn't my style.

But this day had strolled into a free ride on the crazy train. Even for me. The dead guy, this Randall dude, the police station incident and the morgue topped it all. Now I'm probably wanted along the whole east coast for what went down at Mr. Liam's restaurant.

"Man, why is this happening to me?" I really did try to pull my hair out this time as I pulled at the short curls. My natural would need major moisturizing to get me through this. I had to get out of here. I wanted to rush from this creepy place.

"Is everything alright, my dear?" Damn, Randall. I could recognize the distasteful glee in his voice. "Is this not what you asked for? An opportunity for information about yourself? About your abilities?"

"Abilities? You mean killing people with a single touch? News flash, you're a little late. The spider what-not at the morgue did nothing but make me almost crap my pants and probably top the nightmares I already have," I complained.

Randall watched me, eyeing my every move. His freezing hands reached for mine. They were firm, steady to my trembling ones. Way too much to take in. I pulled away and went to stand by the window staring out at the too perfect lawn. Give me the city and cracked concrete any day.

Unholy

If my hand went tingle city on him he'd be the third one within only a few days. No thank you. Spooky things happen when I touch certain people, bad things. And Randall ranked pretty high on my spooky-meter.

I leaned against the window, peering at the moonlit veranda through the thick maroon curtains. I needed to clear my head of all this madness.

"This is a lot to take in," Randall murmured in feigned concern.

Whelp. Misti, time to exit stage left.

I raced for the front door and outside in case he gave chase. I came to an abrupt stop on the porch. Where would I go? Not home for sure. I dropped to the porch on my butt and lifted my head just in time to get hit with a breeze of the cool night air. The scent of sticky pine and wet grass filled my nostrils. I pulled my knees up to my chest and breathed into them a few times.

Footsteps creaked up the hardwood. I assumed it was the guy from the car finally approaching the house probably after another smoke.

"You've got to be kidding me." The voice sighed in annoyance.

Surprised at the harsh words, I lifted my head up to a familiar face. "You're still here?"

"I should be asking you the same thing, girl," Axel shot back. "I was really hoping—which I swore I never would do again—that you weren't here. That by some miracle, you would have run for the hills as soon as you could."

"Yeah? What do you know? This night has been shit, and I have nowhere else to go. This is a safe bet until I can go home without expecting the police to take me away. And don't call me girl!"

I dropped my head back into my lap to escape. *Hello drama queen, so nice of you to return.*

"Hey, quit all that moping and huffing and puffing, Calloway. I know it's getting a bit chilly out here, but if I wanted hot air, I would've went inside."

My lips curled but I kept my answer snarky. "Then why don't you? I want to be left alone."

"Me too," he replied then he sat beside me, leaving little space in between us.

"Seriously!"

"What?"

I take that back. He left no space between us. He was so close to me I could smell his deodorant. He lit a cigarette, exhaling with a nonchalant puff. He finally acknowledged my annoyed glare with an offer of a puff. I declined of course.

"Death by tobacco? No thanks." There were enough things wrong with me. I didn't need to add nicotine addiction.

"Okay, you don't have to be so dramatic."

"Yeah, well, drama and me go way back." I turned away from the horrible smell. But it wasn't enough, so I buried my nose in my shirt. Nope, that didn't do the trick, either. It was as if he was blowing the smoke directly into my face.

I lifted my head and the jerk was indeed blowing smoke rings directly at me. I snorted and scooted away. He was messing with me for shits and giggles but it took everything in me not to give into laughter.

He grabbed my ankle. "Come back. I'll put it out."

I yanked my leg away with a scowl in his direction. I didn't want to go back inside. Didn't want to face more of Randall's mysterious words and freaked out stares.

Axel stood with a stretch and yawn. We didn't speak for a while, even after I saw his cigarette butt flicker pass me into the grass. I tried to keep my cool by slouching against the rail opposite Axel. My eyes traced the pattern of the porch underneath my feet. I shuffled a bit feeling awkward but not able to explain why.

"Randall driven you mad yet?"

"What?" My head snapped up.

"He drives everyone crazy. The general questions and ominous responses, it's the way he is." Axel volunteered. He cocked his head to the side. "So what's your story?"

I slumped my shoulders. "Nothing. Just running into trouble at every turn it seems."

"So you just go around breaking into morgues with some guy you don't know?"

"I-We didn't break into anything," I protested. "Randall had the security code and keys. We wouldn't have been able to get inside if he didn't."

"Hmm, I thought you'd be smarter. Tough chick like you."

I gave him the hand, palm out. "And what does that make you, *Ass-xel*!"

"Touché," he deadpanned. "So what do you do when you're not fighting demon spiders?"

Screw it. I'm in too deep now. "Janitor."

"A what?" When he realized my pause wasn't followed by a laugh, I repeated my title. "Really?"

"And who are you Axel? Are you one of Randall's strays he just plucked from somewhere?" I looked directly at him this time, arms crossed.

"Something like that."

Well that was simple. Not.

"I've been dealing with Randall a long time. Longer than I care to admit." He came closer and leaned against the rail next to me, his back to the house and gaze on the far off distance.

"I know you're freaked out. I'd be freaked out. Randall's legit in his own way though. Just don't let him suck you down the rabbit hole."

Too late. Our eyes met.

"There's something wrong with you but in a good way," he offered with a lift of a dark eyebrow.

Did guys no longer tell girls they had pretty eyes? Talk about shitty compliments. "What makes you think there's something wrong with me?"

When he didn't immediately reply, I assumed he wanted to get his thoughts together to spew more sweet nothings. Instead, he pushed off the porch. He threw his hands over his head and turned his back to me.

He'd changed from the scrubs of earlier and now wore a pair of distressed jeans that cupped a flat butt. The black tee at least gave the lean muscles in his arms a bit of definition. Who knew good old Axel had a bit of a body on him. Nothing like the models on the underwear ads but he looked like a runner or swimmer. Something that tightened and toned without adding bulk.

"There's always something wrong with people like us."

People like us, criminals on the run. I stared back at immaculately cut grass and falling leaves on the trees. "I don't look good in prison orange."

I received a hard kick to the back of my thigh. "Ouch! What was that for?"

The culprit pushed against my shoulder. "Pay attention."

Freaking Axel. His foot poked again before he glanced down at me. "Are you alright? You've had a long night and need some rest. Let me show you to a guest room," Axel helped me to my feet and led me inside.

Wasn't like I had anywhere else to go.

Chapter 7

My eyes opened slowly. Bright light burned through my eyelids speeding up the process. I tried to go back to sleep but something didn't seem right. Newly rested and revitalized, I returned to the living.

"Man, what time is it?" I yawned. Judging by the light outside it was still the early parts of the morning.

Memories from earlier tonight or yesterday, I wasn't sure which, came flooding back like a tsunami. Forget food, my exhaustion and those comfortable sheets. Nothing could distract me from the reasons why I needed to bail on this place. Now.

I figured if I was asleep so was Randall, which would give me the perfect out. The scrubs were long gone but I spotted my sweats and tee shirt on the floor. After I got dressed, I darted out of the room. My sleep-addled brain led me all over the maze that made up the second floor where Axel had shown me the guest room.

I spotted a light shining down the hall. I really hoped it was Axel's room in case I burst in on strangers. I contemplated leaving him without saying bye but he did help me back at the morgue so I owed him at least a heads up. I dug a scrunchie from my back pocket and pulled my hair up in a quick poof. Just because my life was crazy didn't mean my hair couldn't look half-decent.

I opened the door and walked into a fully stocked library. And I admit that even though I was suppose to bounce out the front door long ago, my inner bibliophile imploded when I stumbled upon this treasure trove.

Unholy

I roamed through the center aisles just to see if all the shelves were really filled with books. I even checked to see if it was some image of a spine and title pasted onto an old piece of cardboard. I ran my fingers along the spines of some large tomes in what appeared to be the "Fantasy" aisle, or at least fantasy to me. These books had some kind of rope weaved throughout the entire row of books that piqued my interest. Pulling one from the shelf, the cover had an intricate and elaborate raised engraving with a creature on the front.

Carefully, I cracked open the aged book, turned the first page to a simple title of DRAGONS in delicate cursive font. For the heck of it, I quickly thumbed through the pages to images of what I assumed to be dragons among other depictions of serpents. Something fluttered to the floor as I shoved the book back on the shelf.

I picked up the piece of paper and unfolded it. I studied the faded image of the same dragon from the cover, a lamb and a circle drawing split in two halves. Like semi-circles with one side filled in. Fumbling to return it to its place, the book wouldn't budge.

"Okay, library, what are you trying to tell me here?" I shoved the paper into my pants pocket.

The prickling sensation along my fingertips had me groaning.

"No, not now." Talk about bad timing. The universe really hates me. I wasn't in the mood for this. Not before coffee.

As I cursed the world, I kept my eyes peeled for any strange happenings. I heard murmuring coming from another aisle in front of me. I must have wandered further than I thought and was deep into the recesses of the library.

"Hello," I called softly.

No wonder they hid away up here. I wouldn't want to live with Randall either. I peeked over to the next aisle to see a woman on her knees, sobbing into her hands.

"Hey lady." I stepped a bit closer but kept my distance. No telling what else Randall had going on.

Her sounds were a mixture of sobbing and whimpering. Then she started rocking back and forth frantically.

I blew out a breath and tipped my head to the ceiling. "Hellooo, freak zone."

"I've lost him. Lost him forever," she moaned.

"Who did you lose?" I inched a bit closer.

Her hair was graying on the sides with dark brown trailing behind. She wore an old-fashioned blue smock dress with white polka dots and a petal collar. She turned slightly toward me and asked, "Will you help me find him, dear?"

"Sure, I'll get right on that."

Her sobbing suddenly stopped and for a minute her blue eyes narrowed and turned black. I blinked and they were blue again. "You will?"

"Yeah," I answered and began tossing out names. "Me and Axel and the driver. Oh, and Randall—"

"Don't speak to me about Randall Clark!" She rose to her feet on a shriek. "You're with him, aren't ya?"

I backed away searching for the closest exit. "You hate Randall? What a surprise. Me too. I'll go tell him."

I attempted to move back from her but she followed me forward with every step. I was almost to the center aisle, not realizing how far I'd traveled.

My feet squished, drawing my gaze downward. The carpet was soaking wet but when I looked back up at the woman, so was she. Everything on her, including her hair and smock, became a shade darker and water dripped from her nose.

"Here we go again," I mumbled under my breath. Slowly I inched away to the end of the aisle. The library was far too freaking big.

"You want to help, don't ya, girl? Come set me free. Set me free from this unwanted realm. Allow me to continue to look for my boy Randall stole from me."

Cuckoo went my internal crazy meter. Should have listened to my hand. The hand never lies.

"Yep. Talk to Randall, find your boy. I gotcha." I covered my mouth as if that would muffle my rising panic.

Heavy drops of water plopped onto my head from the ceiling. Water began pouring in a steady stream from above and my only thought was *not the books*. I risked a peek to see the woman now floating a solid two feet off the floor.

Save me the bullshit. I turned back and ran, slamming into a solid form. A hand slapped over my mouth followed by a sharp, "Don't scream."

Axel spun me around and stood between us and confronted the woman.

"You there!" he shouted, pointing.

I gave him the side eye. Was he serious?

"What are you doing wetting up the carpet like this? Keep going and you'll wrinkle these smelly books too."

I smacked his shoulder. "This is a legit library. The books aren't smelly, they're first editions. And ditch the actor dialogue."

Apparently not impressed, Axel ignored me. The woman growled a low, deep grumble. "You shouldn't speak, boy. Randall's perfect little minion."

"Let's play a game," Axel suggested, circling around the hovering woman, squishing and splashing water with every step.

And while he distracted her, I started easing back in search of an exit.

"Hide-and-seek," Axel said. "I figure you're not very good at this game on the count of you losing your boy and everything."

Oh God Axel, don't fucking tease her.

The snarl from the woman agreed with me.

"I would've made it easier for you, but since you don't play *fair* neither will I." The room abruptly went dark.

Shit!

Blinded by darkness, I dropped to all fours and felt for the edges of everything I crawled passed. I heard splashes all around me and coughed when water splashed in my face.

"Axel, Axel?" I called out. I probably shouldn't leave him in here.

"Yes, boy, where are you?" I heard the woman repeat nearby.

Unholy

Change of plans. I rushed to my feet and back to the opposite side as fast as I could but it was difficult with the addition of the thick humid air.

In and out, in and out. I was panting hard in between exhales. I immediately began my mantra. Goosebumps rushed up my body. I could feel her moaning and groaning that raspy smoker's voice in my ear and whispering on my neck as she floated closer to me.

Terrified and disgusted, I started scooting down against the bookcase to the other end.

"I had no choice, girl. They would've taken him from me one way or another. Help me, child. Do what is right. Set me free."

I paused at her plea. "What?!"

I continued to move from the aisle. If I could just find the blasted door. The next thing I know, my face knocked straight into something hard. My lips smashed against my teeth and my nose pressed into soft cotton. I grabbed on.

"It's me," Axel whispered. "You're not gone yet?"

He grabbed my hand and guided me through as if it was no big deal. Our feet squashed with every step. "She's flooding the place."

"No shit. My socks have been soaked in this crap. And that's not the worst part," he added.

Worst part?

"What's the worst part? Cause really, I can't think of anything worst than being stuck in a library with a ghost lady. Oh and it's raining *inside*!"

I got my answer soon enough. Chairs and desks were piled up against the only door out. Axel squeezed my hand tight. I couldn't see him but his grip implied we might have a bit of trouble.

"Truth time, buddy. What does she want with me?"

"What they all want or hope to avoid. Come on, we have to find our way out of here." He let me go and began tossing furniture to the side. I joined in, shoving chairs out of the way.

"Hurry up," I begged, risking a look over my shoulder. "She's not far behind."

He paused with a chair in each hand. "It's not me she's chasing."

I shivered. "I was afraid you'd say that. Go distract her."

He snorted out a laugh. "Yeah, and then what? You, she'll keep and fuck all with me. Me, she'll use as bait to lure you out. Then, kill me."

Like she would really need to use you as bait. At this point, I wouldn't put up a fight if she wanted you first.

"Fine, but work faster."

Our shoulders bumped as we cleared the pile. The mound seemed to grow despite our efforts. I stopped and tried to think of a way out of this.

"Misti, come on," he seethed.

"Let her catch you." I grinned gleefully, remembering how he'd set me up with the spider at the morgue.

"What? Hell no!"

I reached out and came in contact with his back pockets.

"Are you playing grab ass, *now*?" He sounded incredulous.

I huffed. "Let her catch *you*. I have a plan. I think I know how to get rid of her. Run around her. I'll be waiting. Just trust me."

"There's a lot I'd do for you, Calloway, but no."

"Tough shit, Wentz." I shoved him back toward the center aisle and yelled, "We're over here."

I took off at a run in the opposite direction. Well, as well as I could in the ankle-deep water. A scream rang out, igniting my senses making me run faster. I paused and steadied my breathing to listen for any movements from Axel. At first, there was some scuffling but I was relieved at the sound of splashes in the distance. I prayed I was right. I didn't want to cause the loss of another life only hours after the last.

The air was thicker than I remembered. Maybe from the moisture from the water, the closed in library space with no clear way out, my fear for Axel, or a mixture of all of the above. I wasn't sure the lighter I'd pinched from Axel's pockets would work properly so I decided against lighting until the very last second. I only had the one good shot at this.

This has to work. If not it would suck to be Axel.

I climbed the nearest bookcase and waited for Axel to come by with the crazy chick chasing. Soon I heard splashes approach the bookcase but I still couldn't see much. However, there was that stench that seemed to follow her. She was here now.

"You lose, boy," she said, cornering Axel right below me. Her voice was now filled with arrogant victory.

I had to wait for them both to get into position. I listened closely, heard Axel's wheezing pants then the woman.

"Where is she, minion?"

Axel held his hands out to his side. "I wish I knew. No, really. I *wish* I knew."

She raised him above the floor by his collar in her translucent hands.

"Hurry, Misti. Whatever you have planned, do it now." Axel began flailing his legs. I couldn't wait any longer.

I had to make my move. I leaped from my hiding spot onto the woman's back and smacked my palm to her shoulder.

Nothing. "Shit!"

"Shit?" Axel said. "What's the shit for?"

Totally not answering that.

Ghost lady bucked like a wild bronco, shrieking and trying to claw at me. I hung on, legs around her waist. She tossed Axel to the ground and spun in a circle.

With no other choice I went to Plan B and pulled out the lighter, flicked it with my thumb and tossed it on her as I kicked backward.

The only problem? She fell on top of Axel while I was flung away.

Chapter 8

"Misti, what am I going to do with you." I heard Randall through the buzzing in my ears as the water washed passed me.

I can't believe I just did that.

"Axel?" I got up to my hands and knees, looking around. "No, no, no."

He lay a few feet away on his side, no signs of the ghost lady. I didn't bother trying to get up and crawled over. I pushed him onto his back. The water was washing away the soot from his smoking, naked upper torso.

I felt for a pulse on his wrists and neck. Late nights hospital reruns don't fail me now. I banged on his chest a few times. Relief washed over me when Axel gurgled up water and heaved in a ragged breath. After a few coughs, he finally focused on me.

"Hey, man," I said.

He blinked a few times then responded, "Fuck off."

"Well, that's nice," Randall dryly interjected over my shoulder. "Now, if you will excuse us," Randall continued as he effortlessly lifted me from the floor.

My eyes were glued to Axel. He closed his eyes again but continued breathing as Randall hauled me away. My legs wobbled every step. Randall practically carried me out of the damp, darkened library. Axel just lay there. Abandoned.

I tried replaying what happened over and over until my head started to spin. My busy brain had to go poking my nose into something clearly beyond my realm of expertise. I breathed in and out loudly to achieve maximum relaxation to calm my rising anxiety. It was either that or let the drama queen come out to play and right about now even she was scared of all this voodoo shit.

Randall dumped me back in the same bedroom from a few hours before with a stern warning not to wander. Fresh clothes were on the end of the bed. Jeans, a white tee. Even underwear and a bra which made me cringe. Oddly enough, everything was in my size. I couldn't even deal with that yet and fell back on the bed, arms spread wide.

"Really? I can hear you thinking down the hall, but I was hoping it was my charred ears playing tricks on me," Axel said, standing in the doorway.

Axel strolled in looking decently recovered. For a man I'd left semi-burned on the floor, he walked in with ease. And a change in threads too. He pulled back the hood of his sweatshirt revealing the black fuzz on his shaved head. Or was it left over soot? The fire didn't seem to do him much harm. I was thankful and annoyed. He'd scared me to death.

"Over half of your body was burned to a crisp and now you just stroll in." I remained flat on my back when he entered my room and dropped on the bed beside me.

Axel stretched out next to me, placing his face disturbingly close to mine. I could see the brown centers of his eyes and those long lashes he didn't deserve. No guy deserved lashes longer than a girls.

"You're looking considerably pink and shiny these days." Snark was a good conversation started after you'd burned a friend. Was he a friend? I mentally played with it in my head and decided yes. Burning people equaled lasting friendship.

"Is that your way of apologizing?" He folded his hands behind his head, sharing my pillow. *"I have a plan, Axel. Trust me, Axel."*

"I was trying to get us out of there and away from that pyscho." Now that the moment was behind us, I was torn between laughing and crying.

He clenched his jaw. "Look, I'm trying to help you here."

I perched up on my elbows. "How about helping me get the hell outta here. Away from this haunted house, away from Randall?"

He ignored my question and quickly jumped to his feet, leaving me. He stopped in the doorway. "Randall wants to speak with you after you change."

When he left I heard his heavy boots stomp down the stairs. With no other choice, I took the clothes into the connecting bathroom and showered. I dressed in the clothes provided by my kidnappers and skipped down the staircase. I followed my nose to the kitchen.

"Join us, Calloway," Axel called from the table.

Through the door, I saw an extravagant table layout. Candles and flowers, fancy and expensive looking china with gold plated filigree, sharp, clean, and shiny silverware on either side that gleamed at every shadowy movement. Then, my nose breathed in the wonderful, mouthwatering scents of bacon and cinnamon.

Maybe I could stay until breakfast then I'll go.

This beat my measly oatmeal, peanut butter and jelly sandwiches. Axel sat by the end near the door. I started in his direction but his eyes widened in fear and gave a small shake of his head. I debated ignoring him but Randall made the decision for me.

"My dear, come sit by me. The best seat at the table. Well, second best." He chuckled at the head of the table. This time I thought his smile was genuine.

Of course, he would only genuinely smile at himself.

I sat and was immediately served with a cup of piping hot coffee by Randall. Just what I needed. Relished in the liquid gold, sweet and creamy with just the right amount of sugar and hazelnut cream.

"Before we indulge in breakfast. Let's get down to business, shall we?" He sat up straight, flung back his flowing golden mane, cleared his throat and then continued. "I think this is a fine time to finally discuss what's happening. Your friend, Mr. Wentz, only relayed what he could in both the Examiner's office and the library. I'm sure you can give a more detailed and descriptive explanation of said events."

I didn't miss the disappointment in Randall's tone when he eyed Axel and then quickly came back to me. From the corner of my eye, I caught the disgust and anger in Axel's gaze.

I rubbed my damp palms on my pants legs. I did *not* like Randall. "Allow me to summarize. Freaking spider creature in the morgue, weird ghost chick in the library. Both disappeared."

"Well you handled yourself well. Quick on your feet under pressure if I must say." Randall swelled with pride like he'd discovered the latest hit. "And the tingling in your hand, did it not. . .activate so to speak?"

"Um, no. Well, maybe." *You should've trusted your itch, Misti. It's never wrong.*

I didn't think my explanation was as descriptive as Randall would've liked it to be. I don't talk about this stuff with other people.

"Magnificent, truly magnificent." Randall clasped his hands and jumped jovially from his chair. He began to mutter to himself by the window and then, started pacing the floor behind his chair. I stared at him in fascination but felt another pair of eyes on me. Axel. I turned to see him staring intently at me.

"Is that why I'm here, Randall? To solve a ghost problem? I'm not a detective or a spirit medium who goes out and catches ghosts. What do you want from me?"

It was a combination of everything that had transpired that finally made me crack. From being practically kidnapped from my blown-up apartment to being trapped in a dungeon of a library with a suicidal, murderous floating woman hell bent on something.

"Oh no, no, my dear," Randall said softly as he turned to face me. "It's not ghosts I want you to pursue. Those I'm not worried about. I am more concerned about you catching and returning my demons."

I stared at him. "Demons? Like from Hell?"

"Precisely," he answered with a wink.

Creepy fuck. "Cut the bullshit, Randall. What do you want from me?"

"Oh yes, please allow me to explain. I'm just so excited. You have a gift not seen in almost a millennium. How do you think you heard that demon in the morgue? Do you truly believe I just stumbled upon you in that police station? Do you truly believe you were at the wrong place at the wrong time when you had the altercation at the bus stop? No, no, dear. All but Aaron were a test. They were demons and your gift recognized them as such."

I was flabbergasted at what Randall was suggesting. Demons? It was all making a sick sort of sense. I looked towards Axel for guidance but he said nothing. He didn't even look in my direction just down at his empty place setting.

So it's like that, huh? I'm just supposed to figure this out by myself then? Oh, the joys of friendship.

With my hands gripping the tablecloth and the hard sound of my teeth grinding together, I tried to calm myself. I wasn't angry that often since not much could get me to that point. Normally, I would just grin and bear with it until it was over, get through it, talk my way out.

However, I'd suffered one too many mindfucks. "No thanks."

I stormed out of the dining room, through the kitchen, and the front door. The house. Randall. His chummy buddy Axel Wentz. I didn't need this.

I would find somewhere to stay and food to eat. Randall Clark, his demon talk, and Axel Wentz be damned.

Chapter 9

I'd lost count of how many days it had been now. I couldn't risk going anywhere near my place or getting busted by cops who still were probably looking for me. Not to mention the freak Randall Clark.

During the day, I hid in the abandoned home I crashed in. It came equipped with an old fire place which I used to warm up the living room and offer sparse lighting. I was using one of the upstairs bedroom and a blanket I didn't want to think too much about. How did I end up in this situation?

"Jesus," I sighed with another echoing shortly afterward.

"You really know how to live it up, don't ya?"

"What the . . . ?" Recognizing the voice, I jumped up quickly and ran to the window, my escape route already planned.

I hovered on the opened window ledge. The view down wasn't as appealing as it had been when I thought this out. *It's now or never, Misti.*

One, two . . .

On three when I lifted my legs to jump I heard, "Calloway!"

Foolishly, I turned, slipping awkwardly over the edge. Nothing but a *Holy shit, I'm going to die* thought ran through my head. Swiftly, I grabbed for the ledge to keep me from breaking every bone in my body but my sweaty grip wasn't going to hold much longer. The triangle roofing above the door was beneath me but the distance between it and my dangling feet was too far to reach and I didn't want to risk slipping off of that too.

All those catcalls about my "long legs" my ass.

Axel's head popped out, while I hung on for dear life. He grabbed a hold of my wrist to pull me up. I winced but a good tug reeled me in. We struggled a bit to avoid falling all over each other. As soon as I had my bearings, I punched him in the stomach, and shoved. He hit his head hard against the wall. I didn't mean for that, truly, but I didn't have the time to apologize. No one was taking me back to Randall.

I raced back down for the front door. That was the plan. Except for the red and blue lights swirling in front of the lawn. "I. Don't. Need. This."

I backed away from the door, ran for the back but halted in my tracks. Another light darting from side to side outside in the yard. And I was pretty sure my boy, Detective Dennis, would just love to have me back in his sights. I decided the basement would be my only option.

Axel's lean figure appeared at the top of the stairs. He was holding the back of his head with one hand. He glared as he descended one step at a time and unzipped his leather jacket. When he drew near, Axel dropped his arms and folded them over the super hero t-shirt revealed beneath. "Are you insane? Why would you run?"

I waved my hand toward the outside. "Hello? Police, me, wanted. No thanks to you and your buddy Randall."

His look spoke volumes as he scrubbed his hands over his head and snarled, "Count to sixty after I leave, and sprint for the woods over the fence and head for the kid's area. Wait for me."

57

Unholy

I really didn't want to do anything he said but the *unlocked* front door opened on a squeak stopping my response. Axel winced, guilt flashing across his face before shrugging off his jacket and pushed it into my hands. "Wear this, the shirt's too thin."

"Hey, you!" The officer yelled and I took off, Axel going in the opposite direction.

I hit the backdoor off the kitchen at break neck speed, sprinting for the fence. With one foot, I launched myself over. I hauled ass despite the stitch in my side. Shooting down a narrow alley, I leaned against a building with boarded up windows and waited. My throat tight, I puffed wind and thought about how nice a gym membership would have been in my past.

When I felt it was safe I continued on, trying to avoid busy streets until I ended up at Axel's kid's area which was really a worn playground with a broken slide and a swing with a missing chain from one side. There was an old bike trail or walking path with overgrown weeds and cracked stone work. I hunched over in the borrowed leather and slid my hands in my front pockets like it was perfectly natural to take a stroll through at night.

I ventured further and the once lovely trees were now a hanging thicket with branches snagging at my hair. Despite the chill, I was frustrated and sweating like a pig. I sat on a humongous boulder blocking the path and had no desire to keep going. Beneath my feet broken beer bottles were scattered among discarded needles and condom wrappers. Clearly, a bunch of teens and maybe some crack heads came out here. I got comfortable as much as one could on a lopsided boulder in the middle of the night.

I wasn't sure how long I waited before I heard crackling only a few feet away. I braved a glance up at the lone figure approaching, really hoping it wasn't some deviant claiming I was trespassing on his turf. I pulled up the collar of my jacket, hiding my face a bit and zipped up my outer leather.

"Move over," he said.

I scooted over as much as I could before I ended up on the dirt. "How did you get away?"

"Too damn fast. They couldn't catch up to me if they tried." He wasn't even out of breath.

I wanted to laugh. Who knew the skinny, light-skinned boy could run. Axel snapped me out of my contemplation—literally. After maybe his third or fourth snap, I finally noticed he was trying to get my attention.

"My lighter," he said with a cigarette between his lips. "Do you still have my lighter?"

"Oh yeah." I grabbed it out of my pocket and held it out for him.

He cupped his palms around the flame, and took a long drag. He held it, savored the smoke, and then released it. "You might want to get that."

Confused, I looked in the direction he was looking down at and noticed the folded-up paper from the library. I laughed. I couldn't help it. After everything going on, I'd compulsively slipped the paper from my old jeans into the ones Randall provided. I snatched them up and stuffed them back into my front pocket. I scanned the area, not hearing any cops in pursuit. "Do you think it's safe to smoke out here?"

"Don't worry. People come out here to do worst." Then he took another drag, and blew out smoke like a burning chimney to emphasize his point. "Ode de urine. Wonderful."

I bit back a grin. "I meant the brush out here. You don't want to start a fire, do you?"

"How about I promise I won't do anything to this patch of dirt others haven't already done." Axel threw down the lit cigarette by our feet. I was about to say something when I decided he was probably right. "Like I said, don't worry about it."

He rose to his feet and stomped on the dwindling flame. A quiet snick showed he'd lit his lighter. My eyes followed the flame hovering above Axel's face.

"Let's go, Calloway."

He had to be kidding. I braced my hands on the rock behind me and leaned back. "No."

"Come on, Misti," he sighed. "We need to keep moving."

"Not until I get some answers from somebody." I huffed and folded my arms. I wouldn't budge from my spot.

"Really, out here, right now?" His brows lowered, forming a fierce V.

"Yes! Out here, Axel!" I marched over to stand in front of him. So much for not budging. "How do you know Randall? How did you see the ghost or demon or whatever the hell that woman was? Bigger question, how did you even find me?"

Leaves rustled as he moved around. "Randall set me up. This wasn't how it was supposed to be," he admitted. "But, I was and have always been here mainly for you."

That gave me pause. "What do you mean?"

"Believe me, Misti, after everything you've been through, I'm not sure you're ready for that part." I could practically hear the frustration in his voice.

"I'm sorry," I blurted.

"About?"

"You know."

He groaned. "To minimize any further confusion, why don't you tell me?"

"C'mon Axel, I'm sorry about what happened back there, up at the house."

"Which house? The one where you set me on fire or the one where you nearly knocked the shit out of me?"

Hmmm, he had a point. "All of it? And really it's your own fault dragging me there with Mr. Creep factor."

I got the feeling Axel was waiting for more, another explanation, but I explained everything already. What else did he want from me?

I broke the silence. "I'm not going back there. I'm not going back to that house or Randall."

He finally spoke. "Neither am I. Let's get outta here."

"What does Randall want with me? Be honest." I asked.

"Something you want no part of."

"Yeah, I figured that but what is it?"

Unholy

He looked around our surroundings before he responded. "Trust me, it's not something you can come back from."

I knew that feeling all too well. Magic hand plus dead people equal fucked up life. I didn't know Axel's story but maybe it was as bad as mine. Right then and there, I decided to listen, follow, and trust him as much as I could allow. It was the least I could do since I almost killed him.

He led me from the abandoned park to three blocks down the street and around a few corners to a pawn shop. Now I had been through my fair share of dodgy pawn shops but I didn't have high hopes for the ones out here. Most of the stuff they carried was junk or stolen.

"Wait," Axel halted and I almost slammed into him. "Before we go in, I want you to know that there's nothing wrong with you. It's a gift not a curse."

He sounded so sincere. At this point, I'd listen to him because I had a feeling he had a lot more experience with creepy than I did. "Ooo-kay."

We entered the small store surrounded by boarded-up shops on either side of it, and were greeted by an grey haired, older man possibly in his fifties, maybe early sixties. He offered an annoyed and suspicious high eyebrow when I walked in first, followed by Axel. Maybe he was used to but didn't welcome disheveled looking people in.

Or he thought we were here to rob the place which was a likely possibility in this area.

Chapter 10

"We need the book Randall Clark is looking for about his demon problem," Axel announced.

"Whoa, what?" My eyes nearly popped out of the sockets at Axel. Still with the demon talk. He was truly off his rocker. It kinda made me sad since I was starting to like him.

The shop owner suspiciously eyed both of us. His hand lowered under the counter and I had an inkling what he was reaching for. Before the man could draw his weapon, Axel grabbed his shirt and yanked the man down to his face.

"Axel!" I screamed when he jabbed his hand into his pocket only to see him push his lighter and a folded piece a paper onto the counter towards the man.

That's it? We almost got our heads blown off for a lighter and a piece of scrap paper?

Nonetheless, I was relieved when I saw the man place his hands back onto the counter. He opened, and read the paper, then turned his attention to the lighter, looking back up to Axel, fiddling with it in his fingertips. Their heads lowered close together, but I could tell Axel was speaking to him from the way the man's eyes were switching from Axel and then to me and back again. The man's cheeks flushed from Axel's words.

His reaction worried me, so I rushed over to the counter as well. "Look, I don't know what he's told you but we'll get out of your hair now. Sorry to disturb you."

Axel whispered something else and the man's skin went chalky. "No, no, I'd help you if I could but I don't got the book."

Axel let him go and leaned against the counter with his ankles crossed. He made a hand gesture then said, "Find it."

"I'll make some calls." The guy turned his back on us and held his cell to his ear while whispering frantically.

"What did that mean?" I asked, copying the motion with my hand.

Axel smirked. "Reminded him what was at stake."

"Yeah, right. Like a piece of paper and a lighter could explain half of the shit I've been through lately. I wish."

"Are you alright?" Axel nudged me. "You look a bit green. Never seen a gun before?"

"Not one about to be pointed in my face."

My shirt collar tightened around my throat. My palm started to burn, preventing me from saying anything else. Something bad was about to happen, I could feel it. Then, without warning the shop owner ended his call and came rushing from behind the counter. Axel's strong hand gripped my arm and pulled me alongside him toward the back. Not giving me a chance to object, he hushed me, motioning me in front of him.

The owner pointed toward a rug covered with junk, but he and Axel started moving the random items, revealing a hidden hatch underneath.

Someone banged on the front door. Quickly, we rolled up the rug, and the owner opened the hatch, and then motioned us inside to crawl through.

"Get in!" Axel hissed.

"Is there somewhere else we could go?" Nerves shook my voice. "I can't go down there, it's too tight and dark."

Axel pushed me forward without answering. Deep voices rose impatiently, demanding entry from outside. Once down and through the closed hatch, I heard the owner rush back to the front to open the door for the customers.

I glanced around my new nightmare. We were in an underground crawl space of some sort, the walls waiting to devour me I was sure.

"Finally. We've been knockin' forever. You can't be closed, right?"

I froze and Axel's body stiffened too.

"Sorry about that. I had some losers in here earlier looking around but had no money. Made them leave. I must have locked the door out of habit." The shop owner answered in a hurried tone.

"I could smell others when we approached this hovel, but no trace," another voice added.

"They didn't give ya any hassle, did they?" I assumed the owner denied that because the man responded with a, "good, good on ya."

His accent sounded Australian to me but it could easily have been something else, although I was certain it was Australian.

"We heard you were the man to see when we re-emerged," the accented voice continued. "Imagine my surprise when I felt the grimy Earth between my fingers again, the crisp night air breeze over my face once more."

The others murmured their agreement.

Was he a demon too? Were they all demons? And did I actually believe in this stuff?

Axel tapped my knee and flicked his fingers forward, my signal to move. I slowly inched forward, and then stopped to look back at Axel.

He crowded me until we were shoulder-to-shoulder and peered through the cracks of our wooden ceiling. The floorboards rattled with heavy footsteps from above. I tried to keep my mouth and eyes shut from the debris every time they moved but it became pointless. Now I'd have a nice layer of dust in my natural.

"I want to inquire about a book," the Australian speaker said.

"I-I have a lot of books. What kind are you looking for?" the shop owner stammered back.

"Well, *Paul*," he drawled, "this book, I hear, has important information about a certain line. A family that should no longer exist and my friend needs that book."

"I know the book but I don't have it." I held back my snort. Paul sucked at lying.

A fist slammed on the counter, causing me to flinch. "Don't play dumb, you old fool. Give us the book willingly or we'll strip what's left of this piece of shit you call a place of business!"

That man had a similar accent but slightly different. A British influence but not British either. *South African?*

"Calm down, mate. I'm sure our friend here just misplaced the book. No one's come looking for it in a long time, so he has it stashed away from harm. Isn't that right?"

I peeked through the cracks in the floorboards to see all of the men staring at poor Paul, waiting for an answer.

Paul's face paled then brightened with color. "I assure you I don't have that book here in my shop. You must be mistaken or heard wr-"

The leader threw a punch directly toward Paul's gut. I winced as he fell with a grunt, and crouched on the floor holding his stomach.

"Good one, Sam!" one of the three guys said.

"What have I told ya about names, boy!"

The other man cowered back from the reprimand. Then the Australian, called Sam apparently, stooped next to Paul. "We tried it your way, mate. Now, we'll leave a little warning behind in case you *remember* where you put it."

When the scattered stomping and gleeful smashing of glass started above, I turned toward Axel. We bumped into each other headfirst.

"Don't say anything," he warned in a dark tone.

It was the first time he'd ever spoken so harshly and there was none of our usual humor present. The stomps above became a confident stride that suddenly halted above the hatch.

"Oi, now what do we have 'ere?" He jumped onto the rug two or three times.

"Look," Paul pleaded. "I'll look around for the book. Get in touch with your friend if I find it.

"Yeah, well, let's make sure we get our hands on it sooner rather than later or you're going back the hard way."

There was a bunch of laughter following that remark. "Let's go, fellas, we have some hunting to do."

One by one, they all marched out of the shop until the final ding of the front door echoed. I heard murmurs from the owner, glass crunch, and creaks from the floor boards. I tried to move past Axel back out the hatch, but he held me still, and raised his fingers to his lips.

The door jingled again. "I almost forgot. I wanted to see if it was true or not. I'd heard so much about you, but I had to see for myself."

Before I could figure out what the man meant, Axel threw his arms around my head and ears, shoving my face down to his chest. Paul screamed loud and long then silence. I jolted but Axel's hold was ironclad. I trembled, hoping no one decided to check down here. The door opened and closed with a sense of finality.

Axel let me go, my fingers slowly unclenched from his black tee.

"This sucks, Axel."

Chapter 11

Another minute passed before Axel let me out through the hidden hatch. I stayed close as we crept up the four rickety steps. Slumped on his back, arms stretched on either side, Paul rested on the floor. I couldn't see what happened to him due to the lack of blood or injuries.

Axel searched the dead man's pockets and patted down his clothes, his actions brisk and impatient.

"Hey, Axel, quit it!" I ran over to them.

"Would you stop worrying about him? He knows where the book is and wasn't lying about it not being here. He wouldn't be dumb enough." Axel stopped to pace, mumbling under his breath all the while.

"What's the deal with the book? Who wants it so bad and why?"

"It's the history of an ancient line of demon hunters. A family with the rare ability to send demons back through a portal if they crossed over to the mortal side."

I stepped back. Poor Axel. "Riiight. Demon hunters. Portals. I gotcha."

"You can't still be in denial." My face must have answered for me because he rolled his eyes and propped his hands in his back pockets and rocked back on his heels. "Look. Randall found out that there is one descendant left from that family. The book gives the lineage, names, birthdates and everything. It might also have how to contain such a person if necessary."

Unholy

My head was already shaking back and forth in denial. I was slow to the party but I eventually got the invite. "You don't think that I'm—"

"Randall knows about you, Misti. We need that book. *You*," he emphasized, "need that book."

"Okay, so let's say I believe you." Tingling hand, dead people. You didn't need to be good at math to put that together. "What would I do with it?"

He spoke concisely. "Learn how to control your gift."

The truth was sinking in slowly. I started digging through the crap on the counters. Maybe I wanted the book too. "I thought you agreed that the book wasn't here."

"Yeah, but there's got to be something hinting as to where that sleaze ball hid it," he responded.

"Okay, so what should I be looking for exactly?" I asked him, shifting through the odd collection of junk.

"I don't know."

My blood boiled as I turned to face him and threw my hands in the air. "Are you freaking kidding me? We're looking for a book but not sure what kind of book. Oh, let me see, what could it be?"

"Is she always like this?" A voice asked from the corner.

I screamed, leaping into Axel's arms.

He blew out a breath and set me back on my feet. "Finally. Help us find this book so we can get the hell out of here, would ya?"

My mouth dropped open. There was Paul, alive and well. "Wh . . . what? No, there's no way. How the hell is this possible?!"

"Lower your voice, lady. I'm sure you can understand I have a massive headache." He moaned for emphasis.

"You can relax another time. Where is the book?" Axel asked the zombie.

Wait, was he a zombie? I searched him over for any sores or bite marks, but was hard-pressed to find anything since his jeans and shirt covered him from the neck down. My life had become a psycho horror show filled with more twists and turns than a B grade film.

"Are you a zombie?" I had to ask.

"Seriously, Misti. Would you focus? And no, he's not a zombie." Axel directed his attention to Paul. "We need to find that book."

"We need to get the hell out of here is what we need to do," Paul countered.

"We?" Axel's eyes went wide. "You're not coming with us. Just tell us what we need to know and *we'll* be on our way."

I rushed over to Axel and whispered, "Let him come with us. He can help us find the book and maybe help us with figuring out what the hell we need to do to keep me *faaaar* away from Randall."

Axel gripped the back of his neck with one hand. "Now you're down with catching demons?"

"Demons, spirits, zombies, or whatever." I needed answers. This would explain why my life was such a cluster. "Besides, look at him. There's nothing else here for him. Let him come with us. We could use another pair of hands and set of eyes."

Unholy

We stared at each other. *Do it. Please just do it for me.* Axel looked over at the poor man, and gave another sigh. He was going to give in.

"Fine." Axel glared at me. "Paul can help us. What do you know about the demons crossing?

Paul shuddered in relief. "I'm not sure. They've been re-emerging on the surface every few days now. At first it was every once in a while that one escaped, but now it looks like an outbreak. This is just a hunch, but I'm pretty sure it's Randall's doing."

"Right." Axel focused on me then. "We have to hurry and the book is the key."

Chapter 12

"So how did you know about my shop? What else do you know?" Paul inquired.

"I didn't. I was dragged here by Axel." Duh. I turned when I didn't hear any footsteps following behind me. Paul stopped dead in his tracks. The look he gave Axel smoldered.

"What does it matter, anyway? They were gonna come for you sooner than later." Axel pointed out a blue sedan. "Is that yours?"

"Wh-what does it matter? Boy, you didn't think for a second they could've had at least one of them watching the place, looking out for someone who came searching for the book too? Too many demons know who I am as it is."

"You should do a better job on who you deal with then," Axel countered, moving toward the car.

"No honor left among demons," Paul scoffed.

Axel glared. "Misti needs that book."

"Not out here," Axel warned, waiting for the locks to chirp on the doors.

"Shouldn't she already know all, considering who she is?" Paul whispered, tossing Axel his keys and climbing in the back.

"Know what?" Did I look as bemused as I felt?

Paul blinked. "About your—"

Axel slid behind the wheel and stared at Paul. "Not. Out. Here."

"You were clearly dead. What are you?" I asked, in case I was accepting the demon reference.

"Correct, I was dead, but as a part of my condition it's only temporary on this side of the plane."

"Get in, Misti."

I got in the front passenger seat. "Someone needs to explain things to me. All the way. Not just pieces."

Paul leaned between the seats and parted his lips to speak but Axel shoved him back. "All right boy, all right. No need to bite my head off."

More and more curious. "So what can you tell me, Paul?"

"Well, for one don't say names out loud in public. You never know who's listening."

Axel turned a side eye to Paul.

"Why not, sir?" I emphasized.

"Good one," Axel snickered as he pulled out of the parking space.

"Names create a sense of familiarity. No one good demon wants that. They desire fear, intimidation, and respect among their fellow demons. Names means curiosity from enemies and vulnerability," Paul explained. "Some don't care. Those are the ones you need to worry about."

"Do you care, Paul?" I asked him.

"What's that supposed to mean?"

"It says a lot that that gang didn't mind saying your name. Do you care?" I had to ask.

"Mis, don't." Axel intercepted.

I wouldn't let it go. "So, what? Do we speak in code when we talk to each other?" I laughed. This demon business teetered between deadly and silly every second.

"We could just not talk." Axel demanded.

Paul seemed too easily forget my request for more information as we pulled off. The ride gave me time to digest tonight's events.

Is this my life now? Constantly on the run from demons? What role do I play in all of this?

Axel stopped at the end of a block in a neighborhood I wasn't all too familiar with. I joined them, pulling up the collar of my jacket to obscure my face if anyone watched. We marched up a hill, Paul leading the way until we reached a high stone wall with an iron gate at its entryway.

"This is it?" Axel asked Paul.

"This is it."

"A cemetery? The book is in a cemetery? As if running away from the undead wasn't bad enough, now we have to go into their resting place." I whined, glancing around anxiously.

Axel squeezed my shoulder. "It'll be fine."

"I don't want to be out here either. There's always someone watching." Paul chimed in.

Scared much?

"Why would the book be here?" I asked as Paul led us inside through the creaking iron gate.

"It's as good a place as any," he said.

Even though I suggested we bring him along, there was something. . .off about Paul. I followed anyway because Axel seemed to trust this guy and I had nothing else to go on.

"I left it with a guy who used to guard this place from vandals. Whether he's still here or not remains to be seen. We lost touch a while ago," Paul added as we crept along the muddy overgrown headstones.

"Hmm." If I had possession of a book that a lot people wanted, one would think I'd stay on top of where it was at all times. But maybe that was just me.

"Why don't you tell me about yourself, Misti?" Paul paused and glanced back over his shoulder.

I could barely make out his features but something warned me not to be completely honest. "Nothing much to tell. Creepy things happen, I run, I hide then more creepy things happen. Oh wait that's been the last couple of days."

"Yeah, but Rand—"

Axel moved past me and grabbed Paul's sleeve, yanking him in close. "No more questions about her and what she knows. Just concentrate on finding that book."

Okay, now that was definitely suspect. Something wasn't right here, but I had to keep my thoughts to myself for the sake of finding this mysterious book.

"You see that light shining there." Paul pointed it out for us. I could barely see the twinkle of low light flickering through the thick darkness. "There's a small house up ahead for the guard I was telling you two about."

I hunched my shoulders forward as my creepy meter went up. "What about the guard?"

Neither answered and Paul hustled through the broken path more quickly. Axel and I trudged along behind his determined footsteps. When we finally approached the old shack, not house mind you, the light suddenly went out. We all halted only a few feet from the porch stairs. Axel guarded me as he slowly tiptoed toward the porch. Then as quickly as the light went out, it flickered right back on again.

"Quit with the games," Paul demanded from the lone lamp.

"Is the house alive?" I whispered. At this point nothing would surprise me.

Both men looked at me as if I was the idiot.

Were they serious? I snorted. "Sorry. Demons and ghost completely plausible. Dead men walking? No problem. Houses that come to life?" I waved my hand and scrunched my face. "Get outta here. That's a stretch."

Paul tugged at his ear. "I'm not sure how comfortable I am thinking she's *the one*."

Axel sighed and shook his head. He opened the door and waited. "Come on."

I hesitated because…really.

"Misti, the house won't eat you. Promise." Axel's mouth curved in a grin.

I shoved the tips of my fingers in the front pockets of my jeans. "Why? Did it tell you it wasn't hungry?"

Paul barked out a laugh. "The one or not, I like her. Crazy, but I like her."

We entered the house together. When giant teeth didn't spring from the ceiling to snack on me, I relaxed. I glanced around what amounted to an old, dusty shack with sheet covered furniture and boarded windows. This place was freaking me out already and I had the eerie feeling whoever lived here had no intentions of coming back.

"Misti, why don't you rest a bit while Paul and I check out the rest of this place?"

I arched my brows in feigned surprise. "We're using names again?"

Axel glared, I glared back.

"We're in a safe place for the time being, away from prying eyes. At least, I hope," Paul assured, jumping at the reflection of a spider web. Not that I laughed. Nobody liked being caught off-guard by a spider web and that was the honest truth.

Axel ran up the stairs two at a time while Paul and I plopped down on the sofa cushions. We were met with a ridiculous amount of dust that had us coughing and sneezing.

"Is everything all right down there?" Axel yelled down.

"Hazel, the maid forgot to dust," I replied after three sneezes.

Axel returned to us still coughing and wiping dust off. "Paul, did you check in the back?"

"No, I doubt there's anything back there other than more dust, spider webs, and mold," he answered, his face twisted in disgust.

Axel rolled his eyes. "God, you're useless. *I'll* check in the back. You," he pointed at me. "You stay put."

"Sit, Misti. Stay, Misti." I saluted him from my spot.

Axel mumbled something I couldn't catch but I chuckled at the thought of it.

"So Misti Calloway, you're becoming very well-known in my world."

Here we go.

Without Axel to hush him, it seemed Paul was a regular motor mouth. "Rumor has it you specialize in the death of demons and being able to banish them back to Hell or even destroy them all together if you please."

Could I really do that? Is that what this was? I was sending them back to Hell. The tingling in my hands. And more than a few people, possibly hundreds from the underworld knew about it.

I gave him my wtf face. "What makes you think I can do any of that?"

"Young lady, I've met many of the undead re-emerging. Most discussing the fresh air once more as if they're inhaling the heavens themselves. They come to my shop for guidance when they enter this side." Paul paused then, leaned his elbows onto his knees. "The others are scared. The rumors. Randall's quest. Like I said, talk claims you can send them back or get rid of them altogether if you choose."

He scooted closer to me, pushing my comfort zone. His thumbs and knuckles cracked in an irritating rhythm. His intense brown eyes darkened with hypnotic intensity.

"Paul, Misti, back here, I found something." Paul's stare relented after Axel's holler echoed from beyond the living room. We must not have moved fast enough for his taste because stomping up the stairs soon followed.

"Hey, you two." Axel's gaze encompassed both of us. "Come on, I found something you need to see."

Paul didn't say anything further to me, and I tried not to reveal my discomfort to Axel. We all entered the basement and I had to swallow thickly and pretend the closed in space didn't bother me.

The two men hovered over a table, locked in conversation with only a utility lamp illuminating their faces. The basement floor was blanketed with various papers, but they were difficult to read from where I stood.

Paul got done first and promptly commenced a cursing spree of which I took a second to fully admire. Some of the things he shouted would never have crossed my mind but I mentally saved a few for the future.

Axel on the other hand stood against a concrete wall both hands gripping the back of his head and mouth twisted in a grimace. At my approach he shifted placing himself between Paul of the mighty rage-fest and me.

I reluctantly stopped on the bottom step. "What did you find? And why is crazy boy going off?"

Exhaling sharply, Axel dropped his hands to his side. "The book is gone."

As Paul's tirade came to a conclusion involving manic mumbling, I eased down the last step and closer to Axel who was becoming my new BFF even if he didn't know it.

"What do we do next?" I worried my bottom lip.

Paul frowned darkly glancing from Axel and back to me. "The book's gone and my so called friend I left it with is missing."

I took in the ransacked basement. Knocked over shelves, busted door lock and papers strewn about the floor. Yep, no doubt dude was long gone.

Axel walked around, feet occasionally kicking stuff as he stared at the floor. "What makes you think the guard stole it? Maybe someone stole it from him."

"Because," Paul snapped, pointing to something on the wall adjacent to a destroyed table. A mounted cabinet hung by its hinges, the door clearly busted. "That's where it was and now its not. No one else would have cause to look in this shit-hole for anything."

"Come on, big guy," I coaxed, feeling braver than usual. "Can you think of where he'd run? Some place we can track him to?"

Axel gave me an admiring glance. My lip curled in a snarl. Jerk.

"Let me think on it." Paul braced his hands on his hips and continued to survey the damage.

Axel placed a hand at my lower back and pushed me toward the stairs. "Let's get out of here."

I glared at him to show my lack of appreciation for his assist but Paul interrupted us. "I'm not sure your girl should be out and about."

I froze. Mentioning danger and my name was sure to get my attention considering my history. Axel's face took on sudden comprehension and tension vibrated on the air.

"Okaaaay. What does that mean?" And why me?

"Demons are crossing over. More than ever before and all of them are gradually hearing about the one woman who can send them back or truly kill them if she wanted." Paul shrugged. "Might put you on top of the most wanted list if you asked me."

"Shit!" I cursed and yanked on my hair. I didn't fully understand everything going on but it was sinking in quick that I could have a bunch of weirdos on my ass even if I wasn't their new apocalypse.

Paul brightened. "There's a convenience store not far from here. A demon I know pretty well works there. He might know about the book or where the guard ran off to."

"Great! I love the idea of meeting new demons who might have hate at first sight for me," I quipped.

Paul found this hilarious and chuckled after aiming a wink my way. He was growing on me in a loveable, fungus might poison you way. He whipped out his cell. "I'll call my friend."

Axel's brows crinkled. He stepped away from me and picked a few sheets off the floor. "I'm going to see if there's anything here that might hint at the book's location."

"Sure. I'll take Misti with me." Paul slid his phone in his back pocket and clapped his hands together as if it were a done deal.

The coils at the nape of my head curled tighter at the thought of going anywhere alone with Paul. Axel was my security blanket in this new world of crazy happenings and I wasn't ready to let that go yet.

Luckily my sometimes scary BFF agreed. "Misti's not going anywhere with you, Paul. She stays with me."

"Come on, buddy," Paul pleaded, sincerity plastered over his worn features. "I'll take care of her. Plus, I could show everyone how innocent she is and not interested in sending anyone back to Hell."

They both glanced at me.

I raised my hands as if surrendering. "Right, not interested in giving away free trips to Hell."

Axel hesitated. We all knew the final decision rested with him. I sure wasn't thrilled with the plan but what did I know.

Axel shot a dark look at Paul. "You're responsible for her. Bring her back alive."

"Alive?" I squeaked.

I didn't know the opposite was an option.

Chapter 13

"This is insane," I muttered as we trekked to this special convenience store run by a supposed demon no less.

The late night streets of downtown could be scary enough without worry about monsters jumping out at us. I'd take panhandling from toothless strangers over that any day.

"Not far now." Paul sent me a reassuring smile.

I wasn't reassured. "I'll take let's get the hell outta here for $200 Alex."

Paul's lips pursed. I guess he didn't like the reference.

Steam from the construction site next to the store fogged the night air, adding a strong smell of foul sewage mixed with the anticipation of rain. Rain would add a lovely glaze of icing on this crap cake. The only thing keeping me from running for the hills was the fact Axel was tearing that place apart for more clues on how to obtain the book.

We reached a run down store and Paul held the door open as I crossed the threshold. We were the only patrons taking advantage of the store's late night advertised hours.

"Not sure about you but I could eat." Paul promptly ditched me and went straight to what looked like a nacho bar set up in the corner.

After one look at the grimy floor, I grimaced and decided anything I bought would be in its pristine prepackaged container. Why play with food poison if you didn't have to? Then again, he was a demon. I think. Zombie more than likely. Maybe he didn't suffer stomach ailments.

Within ten minutes, Paul met me at the front, arms loaded with goodies. He held a black tray with chips drizzled in cheese and wilted jalapeños. The bored clerk glanced up from clicking away on his cell phone. I raised a brow at Paul and nudged his elbow.

"Not him," Paul mumbled and dug around his pocket until he grasped a hand full of crumpled bills.

The clerk handed back the change and rolled his eyes at me. "Are you getting anything?"

I realized I only held a pack of cookies. I should probably grab something for Axel in case he was hungry. "In a sec."

I hurried back to the aisle barely hearing Paul yell out, "I'll meet you outside when you're done."

Peeking around the shelved breakfast bars, I could see the blurry image of his head outside the store front window. Other than the clerk, the store was empty. I picked up two protein bars as well as the breakfast ones for Axel.

While in the drink aisle looking for something with an energy boost, the door dinged, signaling a new customer. A familiar pinch in my elbow transformed into the burning throb in my hand. The burning progressed to a pulsing beat. *Crap!*

On the big mirror located in the ceiling, I caught a glimpse of a tall man wearing shiny aviator shades and a battered black motorcycle jacket. A sense of foreboding rolled down my spine. I deliberately stayed in the snack aisle. Heavy steps thudded past then backed up. His burning stare met mine through his tinted lenses.

I wish I could see his eyes. Or maybe not. My reflection showed a petrified black girl—wide eyes and fussy natural. My clothes were crumpled too.

The stranger walked closer making no pretense about heading in my direction. I had the brief thought that this could be Paul's 'friend' but the dangerous vibes he gave off didn't reassure me.

His black hair lay slicked back from a broad forehead with a slight ridge. A large nose dominated the middle of his face and thin lips curved up slightly when he noticed my stare. He wore no shirt beneath the leather, exposing vivid tattoos across his chest and neck. Black jeans hugged powerful thighs storming my way. Combined with black boots encased in silver buckles that clicked with every step, I knew I was in trouble.

He slowed as he neared. Our shoulders would bump if I moved an inch. After growing up in the city, I had trained my brain to ignore such behavior. Sometimes you had to play tough. But this was different. I was in a whole other wonderland from the day my path crossed with Randall stupid Clark.

I veered around this guy at a brisk clip to the front where I shoved my items onto the counter. The clerk was nowhere in sight. Suppressing a sigh, I clenched my throbbing hand into a fist, lungs pumping as I waited for the moment for all hell to break loose.

I strained my neck, antsy for a view of Paul who had specific instructions to see to my continued living experience. I heard the familiar *'click', 'clack'* of boots coming my way. He had a huge grin on his face—right before he stopped at the door and locked me in with him.

"You know it's a shame that someone as pretty as you had to get mixed up in all of this."

Paul in his carefree way was chowing down on his nachos with his back to the store. One more reason to kick his teeth in if I got through this. I wondered briefly what the odds of me getting by were.

"Go for it, Misti," my stalker taunted.

Shit, he knows my name! Didn't that mean something?

"Screw this." I glanced longingly at the food as my stomach grumbled and made a bee-line for the back.

Flying past my head, something shiny and sharp almost trimmed my edges. I ducked low and threw my arms up to protect myself. A thud at the shelf beside me drew my attention to the protruding object.

Spikes?

It was long and sharpened to a fine point.

"You really went for it. You've got yourself a really big pair to have done that and really thought you could make it." He laughed. "You can't be the one! Cowering away, all alone like this. You're nothing more than a girl taking on something way beyond your reach."

I wouldn't be alone if Paul was doing his job instead of feeding his fat face. Carefully, I pulled the spike out of the shelf then crawled over to another aisle. His boots echoed as he strolled through the store.

"You know, you make this too easy for me. Do you think that old man is going to help you? And that joke of a 'companion' always by your side—geez how pathetic are they to make you fend for yourself?"

"Who are you? What do you want from me?" I yelled back from my crouch beside a row of microwaveable rice bowls.

"I guess you should know my name. It's Jason. By the way, all of Hell is in a tizzy about you. How that old lady had been haunting that house, in that library for decades. Then you came along and *'poof'* she's gone.

"She got what she wanted. She wanted to be free and that's what I gave her, freedom. What do you want?"

"You idiot, that's not what she wanted. She cries out for help from saps like you so she can kill them."

What kind of house was Randall running? Totally frozen in thought, I never heard tattoo man come into my aisle until a chip bag ruffled beside me. I slowly backed up from the big man and got quickly to my feet to run to another aisle.

"Wait, don't run." His voice was laden with humor. "Don't you want to try and send me back?"

"Not really!" I called out.

He chuckled and the ominous sound echoed off the tiled floors and stained walls. I scooted two aisles over making my way back toward the front and the absent cashier.

"I wish I could believe you but since I can't." He clucked his teeth in remorse.

I hauled tail to the front door only feet away. I grabbed for the lock and handle only to realize he'd torn the damn handle off. Well played, demon stranger.

I banged on the glass to get Paul's attention. His head bopped to some imaginary song and he never looked up as he licked a wad of cheese off of a chip. Another spike flew pass my head and clattered to the floor.

Well, I guess now was as good as time as any to learn to use this gift everyone claimed I had.

"I get the feeling you aren't taking me serious here, Misti."

I turned abruptly, my back to the door to keep my eyes on him. He leaned against the bread aisle, arms crossed over his chest. Wiggling my fingers in his direction, I spoke in a confident tone. "I got rid of the lady as you said and I'm sure I can get rid of you too."

Sheer bravado but with my back-up feeding like a pig in a trough I had no choice.

"Ooohh." He faked a shiver. "It's a good thing I like to play with my food before I eat it; despite what my poor mother used to say."

I couldn't imagine what she had to put up with; poor mother indeed.

"Well, I'm done talking." I thrust my arm forward. It tingled, burned but nothing happened.

A wrinkle creased his brow. "I guess you like to play too."

He straightened from his pose and the next thing I knew he hurled another spike at me. He was quick, I had to give it to him. So quick, when the spike skimmed past my face I felt air brush my cheeks. I dropped to the floor and the spike imbedded in the wall behind me.

Unholy

I raced for the back all the while cursing for letting Axel and Paul convinced me that I was some super gifted chick. I searched for something hard to throw and scooped up several cans of soup. I hurled them at the door from my hiding space but the glass didn't shatter. Probably reinforced thanks to vandals in this area.

"Now you're catching on," he crowed with a broad grin on his lips. "You're beginning to earn my attention now."

But I wasn't through yet. I decided to screw the mystic stuff and play to my strengths—staying the hell out of the way. As quickly and precisely as I could, I threw one can at Jason then another. I repeated this until I ran out of soup cans and moved on to soda next.

Jason sent another spike my way, nearly amputating my hand. I jerked out of the way in time and it hit the stack of soda cases, causing them to spill dark liquid over the floor. Sparks exploded above me making me step back from the liquid, in fear of electrocution.

"You're just making this harder for yourself, girl."

Don't call me, girl.

Again, I started hurling cans at him. Anything to delay as long as I could in hope Paul lifted his head and spotted the demon about to demolish me.

"Stay still damn it!" Jason sounded more frustrated than amused now.

He was throwing spikes aimlessly around the small store every time he heard any sudden movements. Snacks, soup, and soda spewed all over the floor. I didn't know how I could get close enough to try the door again without alerting him. I was down to my last soda bomb, a two-liter, and I would have to use both hands. I snuck a look at Jason. His aviators were gone now and his jeans were soaked. The leather jacket hadn't faired any better with the splatter effect of my attacks running down his sleeves.

"I don't hear you, Jason. Getting tired? Not so tough now, are you?" I tried to bluff and stall.

"I could go all night, bitch. You're not getting out of here any time soon. You can throw all the items you want, but no amount of time is going to get you out of here tonight. I have forever."

I had no doubt about his immortality, but his voice sounded pissed. Apparently I wasn't as easy a target as he'd expected. I grabbed a smashed chip bag and intentionally over threw it behind Jason. A spike speared the bag midair raining slivers of chips everywhere. The bonus came when the spike went straight through, crashing through the thick glass door's window.

Without hesitation, I angled the soda bottle while on one knee up and the liquid shot toward his face. I jumped out of my spot and threw a double-fisted punch into his abdomen, and jumped onto his back.

Jason roared and shook like a wet dog. I flew through the air and hit the floor. Pain radiated up my back but I crawled to all four and stood.

Jason took quick, deep breaths. I couldn't help but mimic along with him. The anticipation was killing me, but I didn't have to wait long for what was to come. He shrugged off the jacket. Shiny tips of metal protruded from his chest growing from studs to slender spikes which pierced through his torso. The longer ones were almost the size of the ones he'd thrown at me. His breaths had grown louder and the more they did, the more I realized he wasn't taking deep breaths but was laughing so hard he was shaking.

"Are you ready for the real fun, Misti? I am." His wicked grin stretched across his pale face.

Chapter 14

At least we'd gotten Paul's attention. He dropped the nachos or at least the black container because it was empty. Paul pressed his hands to the glass, his face sheathed in terror.

"Come on now, you've had your fun. Now it's time for mine." Jason's tone remained jovial but his voice became deeper and raspier than before.

Half-running and half-stumbling, I tried to dodge back into one of the aisles. Jason ruined the attempt by lifting the entire row of shelving, and threw it easily above his head. Right then and there, I saw Jason for the true demonic monster he was inside. He hunched over, giving feral growls after each breath he took. He still had that disgusting grin across his face and his eyes now glowed red.

"You can't handle those like me from Hell."

Banging continued against the front glass window. Paul was finally with the program and throwing something against the door to try to break through.

"Don't worry," Jason hissed to me. "I'll be done with you before he gets in here. I have my own business with him to attend to later."

He stepped closer to me, the spikes poking through his skin becoming longer with every step. Lacking any other way to avoid him, I threw myself at his legs, wrapping my arms around them. He tried to awkwardly shake and wiggle me off but I held on for dear life. The horror of what would happen if I let go caused me to tighten my grip on his calves. I got turned around enough to witness Paul's frantic efforts. Our eyes met, and he stopped mid-bang.

Don't stop now, idiot! Instead I yelled. "Paul, get me out of here! The handle's broke. He broke the handle!"

Paul banged on the glass. "Misti! Misti!"

I resisted the urge to roll my eyes. Clearly I wasn't going anywhere. Jason managed to shake me off with one violent kick and I skidded across the gross floor and certain death by germs.

The demon faced Paul and a series of spikes launched at the door. Paul ducked low and ran off.

"Mother—", I bit off the curse in disbelief. I couldn't believe this but why was I surprised. Jumping to my feet, I clenched my hands at my side and decided running wasn't working.

Jason took a giant leap in my direction and hoisted me in the air by my throat. I choked, hands locked around his wrist in vain.

"How does it feel someone else can control your fate, Misti? Did Axel really think he could protect you?"

Mentioning Axel sent a surge of adrenaline through me. I fought harder and dug my nails into his skin.

Jason leaned in close, his fetid breath blowing in my face. "This time I'm sending you away and unlike demon kind, you won't come back."

A loud bang interrupted his prepared kill speech. Dude was monologing. I snickered.

"I'm going to kill him first then you." Jason sneered as he tossed me to the floor.

I fell, gasping for breath as I dragged air into my lungs. Jason turned toward the door and I could see Paul using a shovel and prying at where Jason's spike had penetrated. His arms reared back and plunged forward, sending glass shards exploding everywhere. At last.

"Misti, hang on!"

Right. All over that, Paul.

Knowing I didn't have much time, I planted my feet and launched myself at Jason's lower half, avoiding the spiked torso. For the first time ever I wasn't afraid of causing death. I planted my hand on his right thigh, took one breath and dug deep for my curse/gift.

Come on, come on. Weird ju-ju don't fail me now.

My hand tingled, giving me hope. Another strong surge had me giggling in relief.

And for once my palm lit right up, no hesitation.

Jason reared back, contorting at a twisted angle. I wanted him down completely, at least long enough until Paul could get all the way in. I pushed through the lingering tightness in my throat and squeezed my fingers around the fleshy party of his leg.

"Did you think I'd go back to hell that easy?" He snarled and yanked my head up to face him.

Glass crunched as Paul raced toward us. My palm burned but I didn't lose contact. He was weak now. Weak and vulnerable. My lips pulled back and I pushed more energy through my hand. I met his gaze and smiled. "Tell your friends, I'll be waiting."

Disbelief crossed his face as his body began to fold in on itself. Light filtered through cracks spreading across his spiked skin.

"It won't end with me," Jason screamed moments before he vanished.

I sagged to the floor as Paul caught me about the elbows. "Shit, I don't need to worry about you sending me to Hell. Axel is going to kill me."

"Forget Axel," I muttered, trembling. "I'm going to kill you first, you nacho eating loser."

Paul hurried me outside. At least he kept an arm around my waist to help me along. I couldn't believe I'd gone toe-to-toe in a battle with a demon. And won. Holy shit! I won. A stupid grin spread over my face and I didn't care that it was probably an adrenaline high. Right now I felt like a winner.

"Why didn't you scream for help when the demon attacked?"

I looked at Paul. "Really? Are you serious?"

He sputtered and I recognized the streets back to the cemetery. "You have to believe me, Misti. I didn't hear anything until the end. I was hoping to catch sight of my friend."

"While eating nachos?" I snorted and straightened to walk on my own. I didn't hurt too badly but some pain relievers would be great.

Chapter 15

"Step lively, Misti!" Paul puffed as he upped his pace.

Without looking back, we raced toward the cemetery's iron gates. Paul pushed me in and I heard the metal clash together as he slammed them shut behind us. I pressed my hand against the cramp in my side. I was far from a track star and our trek after my fight wore me out. I maneuvered through the darkness with only the dismal porch light in the distance to guide us.

Weaving in, out, and around grave slabs, and head stones, ducking low tree branches and roots sticking like long legs out to trip me. I paused by one tree to gather my bearings but Paul sped up and left me behind.

"Hey, wait!"

Soon I could no longer see him and fear returned with a vengeance. I tried to pick my way through. Fog thickened about my ankles. I could make out Paul's burly figure continuing with no clue I wasn't at his side any longer. He sucked as a guardian figure. A few moments later a door opened and closed, signaling Paul was inside.

Huffing in annoyance I hurried forward.

At least he's safe and sound. Now what about me?

Moments later he poked his head right back out. The man who left me to a demon's mercy while he ate nachos and almost lost me in this graveyard was actually looking for me. Instead of calling out, I walked faster. At this point, I only wanted to get back to Axel.

Unholy

Paul whistled a birdcall a few times and my eyes rolled though no one was around to appreciate my irritation.

Probably should use the bat signal. "Cuckoo!" I called out to be smart.

That got his attention. He pivoted back and forth between the small porch and the closest gravestone. I assumed he was waiting for Axel to appear since he kept looking back at the door. It was either the darkness on my end or the fog on Paul's because both made me blind with frustration and anger rolled into one. I kept knocking into headstones and tripping over rocks on my way. I didn't remember it being this treacherous on our way in the last time.

When I was feet away from the porch, a relieved grin crossed his face. "There you are. I thought I lost you."

My foot snagged on a root or something before I could take the final steps. The more I tried to untangle my foot, the worse it got. My nice shoes sunk deeper into the ground caking mud around my ankles and sliding into my socks.

"Hurry up!" Paul snapped added a frantic hand gesture. "It's not safe in the dark out here."

"No kidding," I muttered under my breath and bent down to free my foot.

I was almost loose. So close. That should have warned me. My night had been hell from the start. Not the real Hell but the emotional one.

Grimy, dirt-filled, broken fingernails attached to boney hands burst through the dirt and flexed in the air then retreated back into the surface.

"Shit! Shit! Shit!" I glanced up. "Paul!"

He stared, mouth falling open.

What an idiot!

Another ghoulish hand shot up beside me, reaching for my sleeves and then, another by my stuck foot. They clawed and groped at me, dragging me down toward the ground. I lost my balance and fell on my butt. Dampness soaked through the cotton.

"Misti, Misti, where are you?" Axel came out, joining Paul on the porch.

"Axel, help!" I had no shame.

"What the –?"

Axel leaped to the bottom of the porch steps, but Paul pulled him back. "You can't. Those are the undead."

The hell he wouldn't. My gaze locked on Axel. "Come on. We're in this together remember?"

More hands clawed at me yanking me hard enough I fell onto my back.

"Let me go. They're going to take her if we don't help," Axel yelled.

I struggled more as my terror began to take over. This wasn't funny. Not in the least. A bony arm clamped about my waist and dirt started to cave in about me as I fell beneath the moist Earth.

This was it. When I thought of my death, I never imagined I'd be buried alive. The world faded to black as a layer of soil covered my face and blocked a fighting Axel and Paul from my view.

When I opened my eyes again, I was in an underground tomb. I blinked, my eyes adjusting to the darkness. Cautiously, rolling onto my right side, I pushed up to a squat and then stood. Everything hurt.

"Mis-ti." Two scrawny demons with sunken faces and skeletal limbs approached me with lurching steps.

"Oh shit. Oh shit. Oh shit." I jumped up with a wince.

"Mis…ti."

The moaning of my name was not working for me. I held up my hands. "Look guys, I'm not interested in sending you to Hell. So run along with you."

I made a shooing motion with my fingers. They jerked and I wondered if I could scare them into leaving me alone. Then I heard it. Low fierce rumbles.

My demon friends vanished and I was left in the darkness. By myself.

As soon as I had the thought. A row of torches lit themselves, one after the other. The nearest wall was lined with the burning sticks.

I needed to find Paul and Axel.

"Hello," I called out weakly.

The room had all the elements to make it a fitting dungeon. Dirt or possibly clay floors-check. Cobble stoned walls, and ceiling-check. We just needed a medieval torture dude to complete the picture.

There was a stone roundtable in the center of the room with another half-circle stone-like bench to the side. I spotted a tunnel behind the two stone structures. As creepy as the thought was, it was possibly my only way out. I lifted the closest torch and walked over toward the dark tunnel.

"Hello." I called out again, this time with a stronger voice, pretending I wasn't shaking like a twelve year old during recess about to have his ass kicked.

This time, no torches reacted. Below me I spotted something reflecting in the light. I recognized the familiar design. I thought back to the paper I'd found in the library at Randall's house.

Distant snarls and growls had me huddling against the wall as renewed fear leaped to the forefront. Whatever it was must have been deadly in order to scare off those demon things. The sounds grew louder as I eased backward and tripped over something. Turning, I found a narrow stairway leading upward. Tough choices—wait for the strange, hidden monster or go toward the unknown.

Neither option appealed but I followed my gut and went with the stairs. The steps spiraled in the middle, uneven risers making me take extra care. Ahead I recognized Paul and Axel screaming my name. Mainly Axel.

Thank all the powers to be and then some. "I'm here."

At the top of the landing, I set the torch aside on the small ring formation to the left of the wall. I faced a thick door with deep carvings in the grain of the wood. Heavy fists pounded against it.

"Misti, is that you? Open the door."

Axel and his demands but still I grinned in relief. "What do you think I'm doing over here?"

I gave the metal handle a good pull as if to demonstrate my point though they couldn't see.

"On the count of three, we'll both push and you'll pull," Axel instructed.

Our combined efforts managed to move it a bit each time. "It's working!"

101

Giggles escaped but I was too damn glad the door opened enough for me to shimmy through.

"Oh, thank God, Misti! Thank God you're okay." Axel wrapped me tight in an awkward hug. "Come on, we need to get out of here. If Jason found you at the convenience store, another will soon be on its way here."

I glanced around and realized we were in the basement of the shack in the cemetery. Still wrapped in his unbelievably strong lean arms, he asked, "What happened? How did you get down here? We saw you get dragged—"

I cut Axel off. "Trust me when I say I know what happened."

He glared and I gave him dark look for dark look but Paul interrupted our stand off. "Is anyone else curious how she got from the dirt hole to this basement?"

Paul received my renewed glare but merely shrugged. I gave in. "Down those stairs is a room."

"Leaving here since we didn't find what we came for is better than searching a musty room, Misti," Axel suggested.

I wanted to agree with Axel but this might be important. I dug in my proverbial heels. "I'm fine, Axel. We can go after you both see what I found down the stairwell."

Axel begrudgingly agreed with an abrupt nod. We turned as one unit and all went down. I made sure to stay in the back since I'd had enough creep factors for the night.

"Oh. Wow!" Paul reached the bottom first, walking over to the stone roundtable.

"There's not much here," I explained. "But I thought the design was worth another look." I pointed toward the carved lines in the wall.

"You stay out of the way." Axel lifted one of the wall torches from their mooring after giving me the order while Paul grabbed another. They both leaned forward to study the symbols.

I leaned a hip against the wall to give my tired feet some slack and to wait for the verdict. "When you guys are done, there's something else I wanted to show you," I called out. Neither bothered to glance in my direction. Figures.

"Hey, did y'all here me—"

The growls and snarls from earlier returned but this time a dark shadow soared across the space before any of us could react. Axel spun away but Paul dropped his torch and screamed causing the creature to charge after him.

"Fuck, the little fucker bit me!"

Axel kicked out and dragged Paul back. Blood dripped from his hand to spatter the floor.

"What the hell?!" I straightened and tried to see through the dark wavering light provided by Axel's remaining torch.

"It's over there," Paul screeched, pointing.

A pair of evil yellow eyes glowed. A beast of some sort? It bared fangs at us.

"Why didn't you tell us that thing was down here?" Axel demanded while he tried to calm Paul down. I ignored him, more intrigued by the…dog?

Unholy

Axel aimed his torch in the direction of the snapping barks. A small black dog, a puppy really, crouched in the corner. The hair on its back ridged up. It looked more afraid of us than we were of him. Kinda. Of course I was a dog person so that may have impacted my clarity for the moment.

I limped closer to the fur ball. "Hey, baby. We're not going to hurt you."

"Let me get close enough and I will hurt him."

I wanted to smack Paul but kept my attention on the now whimpering animal. "Awww, you didn't mean to hurt him, did you?"

It cocked its square head to the side and the tiny pointed ears perked up. At least the growling stopped. I went down to one knee and extended my hand palm up.

"Misti, you better know what you're doing," Axel cautioned.

"Yeah, yeah," I muttered, my gaze still on the puppy as it came toward me.

"Does anyone care that I'm bleeding here?" Paul wailed.

I ignored him too just as the puppy licked the tips of my fingers then jumped into my arms. I laughed and cuddled it close. Hadn't expected that.

Axel sighed. "I guess we're adding a dog to the mix."

I smirked and stood up. "We're like our own band of kick ass heroes. This here is our mascot."

"This is ridiculous." Paul pouted as he complained and held his hand to his chest.

"Like being chased by demons isn't?" I asked. "Anyway, you'll be fine. Remember the mysterious zombie-like condition that made you perfectly fine when you woke up from a critical injury."

My snark shut the both of them up. Holding the puppy, I found myself full of confidence. I looked at Axel. I mean, really looked at him. If you don't ask now, you'll regret it my inner voice warned. "What are you anyway?"

"What?" He frowned and cocked a single brow at me.

I wasn't fooled by his feigned confusion. "Don't. Randall can do it, these demons who want me dead can, hell even Paul can, but not you, Axel. Don't lie to me."

We couldn't be BFF's if he did.

Axel rubbed the back of his neck then scratched the back of his crew cut head. I waited for the answer he clearly didn't want to give. "I'm, I'm…not…human if that's what you're asking."

"I know that. You can't be after all that's happened. Me setting you one fire, you always popping up around me. That's clearly not human. So again, what are you?"

His jaw tightened. I shook my head, and headed toward the stairs. I was supposed to trust this guy with my life and he couldn't even trust me with the smallest detail about what he was.

"Do you know anything about your family history, Mis?"

I stopped willing to give him a chance to explain.

"I once worked under, well, more like was enslaved by a witch." That made me perk back up. "I'm what one would call a familiar. We're normally bonded to a chosen line but in my case, I was a slave. Cursed to work for a witch for her entire mortal life. When she died I was released from her control. The day she took her last breath, I was elated. I couldn't remember the last time I was happy about anything."

"What happened when she died?" I asked.

"She told me once she died I would be free to move on. Maybe find the chosen line I belonged to but in death she fucked me over. When a witch or sorcerer dies, all their possessions go to whoever they were in debt to. This ended up including my contract of servitude."

Holy crap. "Randall has something to do with it, doesn't he?"

"Yes. He became my new owner when she died."

I didn't have a good feeling about where this was going. I spit out my next words. "Just finish it already!"

He licked his lips and locked his fingers behind his head as he paced. "Randall wanted me to make sure you completed your tasks at the morgue and again in the library to prove what he someone how discovered. I was to convince you it was okay to listen to him and join his ranks. I wasn't allowed to tell you anything about your powers or your gift to send demons to Hell. None of it. You were difficult and ran off so he told me to kill you."

That made sense. Randall was definitely a you're either with me or against me kinda guy.

Axel choked out a laugh. "And I was ready to do it. I was ready to lie, cheat, steal, if it meant my freedom. Which he promised if I helped him. But the moment I met you I felt the connection. You're from the family line the familiar in me is supposed to bond with. I knew I couldn't let Randall kill you when I realized."

He took a deep breath, then closed the gap between us. My new guard puppy growled.

"You're in Randall's way, Misti. Because of your bloodline. You are descendant from one of the most powerful demon hunter families ever born. When I realized what Randall wanted to do, I knew I couldn't trust him to stand by his word." Axel snorted. "Plus you were proving to be foolish and a danger to yourself."

I flipped him the finger and bit my bottom lip to keep from smiling. "Thank you for the truth."

"Me too." Paul sniffed and wiped a tear from his eye. "That's the most moving story. Man, I want a group hug."

"Ew, no." I cringed away. Then what Axel said fully hit me. Finally I believed everything they were telling me. I was a demon hunter. "I can get rid of Randall, right? I mean he is a demon after all. Will I be able to free you?"

"Let's not jump too far ahead of ourselves. We need the book to train you on how to control and use your powers."

I rolled my eyes but mentally agreed.

"We need to crash for the night." Axel glanced around. "Not here but I guess the guard's shack upstairs is as good a place as any where Randall won't find us yet."

As we returned to the upper levels, Paul spoke. "I guess this is a good time as any to confess to the fact there's a bounty on your heads."

We crossed over from the underground room into the basement of the shack. I smacked Paul on the shoulder. "Really? You waited to tell us now?"

His sheepish grin did *not* amuse me. "Randall really wants to stop you if you're not on his team. You could ruin his plan to have demons overrun the place. Of course your boy, Axel, is on the shit list since he essentially defected."

The puppy wiggled in my arms so I set it on the floor as soon as we were back in the main part of the house.

"There's more."

Axel slammed the basement door closed behind us and we entered the living room. "With Randall there always is. Get it all out, Paul and it better be everything."

Paul held his arms up. "Hey, your confession compelled me to be honest too. I may have told Jason Misti would be at the store."

It happened in a blur. Axel ran toward Paul and punched him in the face. "I knew it! I knew it was too easy that he found her there after you begged her to go with you."

My puppy got in on the action and nipped at Paul's ankles. I pushed between the fighting men and separated them. "I get it! I get it! Paul is a jerk but he told us, Axel. Stop!"

Chest heaving, they broke apart.

"Fine," Axel snapped. "But if he does anything else to betray you again, he's dead."

"No way, man. I'm on the straight path now. We find the book and train your girl here then kick Randall's ass."

It sounded like a good plan but nothing so far went according to plan.

Chapter 16

"See, I told you if we took the light rail straight down it would lead us straight here to the terminal port dock."

"Yeah except for the part where you had to pretend to be blind so we could get on the bus instead of huff it all the way over here." Axel added.

"Hey, if you wanted to walk over instead, you were more than welcome to. But, I didn't here you complain when you started snoring on our trip here."

I snickered when he decided to ignore that bit. We were lucky to even get a bus to take our ragged crew. The big stick I found outside the cemetery added a nice touch to the blind act though. Hopping in and out of cabs and trekking everywhere on foot with a vivacious puppy was an exhausting no for me this morning.

"What now?"

When we woke the next morning at the shack, Paul claimed to have an idea on where we could find the book before Randall got his hands on it. Apparently there was a section in it, which spoke on how to end a demon hunter or render me powerless. I definitely didn't want Randy-boy to have the book in his possession after hearing that.

"*He's* here," he answered simply.

"*Who's* here?" I glanced around all the large multi-colored crates which littered the port. "There's nothing more than crates here. What could possibly. . ." I turned back to Paul who had a smile spread wide across his face. "Oh no."

More demons. I didn't need him to spell it out.

"Don't worry, Misti," Paul cajoled. I commenced to worry. "The guy here can help us find the book. He's the go to for any information in the demon underground."

"If you're lying, I'll have Milo take you out." To support my statement, the black dog latched on to the cuff of Paul's jeans. Man, I should have gotten a dog a long time ago. They were great.

"You named the dog Milo?" Axel stared in disbelief.

"Um, yeah. It's a cool name."

"That name is ridiculous, like you," he teased.

"Oh yeah, and what's a name like yours then, *Ass-el*?" I elbowed him hard.

After everything I'd learned the night before I was glad we were back on even footing. We continued down the paved walkway in search of Paul's mythical friend who I hoped could help us.

Milo's sudden bark startled us as he took off for a stack of wooden boxes piled high and neatly lined up against a gigantic steel structure several yards from us.

"Good boy, Milo! Did you see that?" I didn't know what this was but it was a good opportunity to highlight Milo's ability to help us since Paul and Axel thought I should have left him abandoned in the cemetery. Cruel demons.

Large, jagged scratches marred the steel. Axel leaned in closer and we all noticed there were more tears going up the side.

"What could have made marks like that?" I asked.

"I'm more worried about how fresh they are." Axel smoothed his hand slightly across the surface. I could tell when the answer hit as his gold skin tones paled.

"What is it?" Against my better judgment, I reached for the marks myself.

Milo barked, lunging for my wrist, and Axel yanked me back by the leather jacket. "No!"

"Ooo-kay." I raised my hands in the air and eyed him carefully.

Paul kneeled beside us. "If those are what I think, it's best you not touch 'em, girl."

When the traitor demon and your good friend demon agreed on something, it was best to listen.

Axel's grip on me loosened. "What else do you see?"

It took me a moment. I wasn't up on my demon protocol yet. "They. . . they don't . . . come . . . back down?"

"They don't come back down," he confirmed. "What kind of creature do you know who can climb up this big ass steel crate, make multiple on the way to the top, but never come back down, creating drag marks instead?"

He stared at me knowing damn well I didn't have an answer. I just stared stupidly at him and back at the marks going up the crate. Axel backed away from the boxes far enough, sizing up how high they were.

"How do you plan on getting up there? There's no way you could climb up there yourself."

"It's not impossible." He toed off his shoes and his socks right after.

"How about we try the door instead?" I suggested.

"I'd rather be on top then trapped inside any day."

No, that didn't sound suspicious at all.

"While you're up there," Paul added. "I'll go look around for my friend and meet back here in fifteen."

His suggestion had sketchy written all over it but Axel and I agreed and Paul trudged off at a brisk clip.

I waited until he was well away from earshot before speaking to Axel. "Do you think that was a good idea to let him go off like that?"

"No." Axel maneuvered in position and started to climb the structure. "He tends to disappear when things get hot."

After the convenience store incident I couldn't really argue with that. "At least he's making himself useful instead of stuffing his face this time."

The further Axel climbed the more I inched back to keep him in my field of view. I made suggestions whenever he paused in his advancement but these were met with a harsh curl of his lips so I gave up and waited. For two minutes.

"Almost there," I yelled in encouragement. Another few minutes passed and Axel was a dark blob, moving upward at a pace I could never match. I glanced around for any signs of Paul returning.

Milo snarled at my side, drawing my attention to Paul jogging down the path back toward us, hands waving in the air. He grabbed my elbow and tugged when he was in reach.

I dug my heels in and swatted at his hand but he wouldn't let go. "What's with you?"

"We gotta get outta here. They spotted us." He huffed in between explanations, continuing his frantic pulls.

Goosebumps broke out on my arms. "Who? I thought you wanted us to see your *friend*."

"Yeah, well apparently he's got company. Bad company."

I looked up, hoping to tell Axel but he was too far away to call without drawing more attention.

"Misti, we really need to go," Paul begged.

I searched behind him and beady read eyes peered back. Oh, shit. I let Paul pull on me as Milo let out a fierce series of barks. We ducked behind more boxes, crates and things waiting to be loaded. I grabbed Milo by the ruff and hushed him.

"This way, Misti." Paul released his death grip on my arm and raced ahead.

"Damn it! Wait!" I glared as his retreating figure vanished down the narrow passageway.

I debated chasing him when a noise pounded from inside one of the nearby crates. Maybe I should go back to get Axel. The pounded echoed around me again, setting Milo off on another round of barking. Pulse thumping, I walked back the way I came, my gaze never leaving the noisy crate which was now emitting a nasty, low growl in a continuous rumble.

"Milo, we need to get out of here."

My faithful companion stayed beside me as we made our way. Pounding came from another crate behind me and I gave up stealth and dignity to scream. "Axel!"

Unholy

I burst back onto the main path only to be confronted by the owners of the beady red eyes. I came to an abrupt halt. "What. The. Hell?"

I jerked around but couldn't find Axel. Milo leaned against my leg snapping and growling. These creatures were way bigger than my dog. And there were three of them crouched over in ragged clothing. Long toe nails bared by the lack of shoes began to paw at the ground leaving deep jagged marks in the concrete. Familiar marks.

Charcoal skin with smoke rising from every inch covered the lanky frames of the...things approaching me. Bald, ridged heads swiveled back and forth as spittle dripped from the distended jaws. The drops hit the claw marks and smoke rose from the ground. Well, that explained why no one wanted me to touch the marks. Guess Axel was demon proofed against getting burned.

The three creatures formed a semi-circle, blocking me from getting back to the exact spot where I'd left Axel. Milo leaped in front of me, head tucked low and hair bristling along his spine. My hand burned and I almost cried in relief to feel my curse gearing up.

"Unless you want a one way ticket to Hell, you might want to leave."

The one on the far left licked its lip with an ugly black tongue, swiping from cheek to cheek. I grimaced because that mess was nasty.

BANG.

The explosion from behind had me dropping to my knees and cowering. The beady eyed things spun to face this new threat and I watched the pathway where Paul had ditched me.

Another demon lunged forward, its skin a shiny alabaster. The three in front me exchanged looks and clicked to one another. Whatever they said must have set off the lone demon because it screeched and jumped forward attacking all three at once.

"Milo, let's go!" I stood up and took off despite the quaking in my knees.

I clenched my hand into a fist at my side in case any of them thought to stop me. I'd burn those bastards back to Hell so fast they'd think I was an expert demon hunter. The noise behind me turned to squeals and screams. I risked a glance over my shoulder and the lone demon was kicking ass, tearing into the other three and splattering blood and gunk everywhere. Smoke rose from the ground where the stains landed.

I skidded by the boxes Axel had climbed and chewed my bottom lip. Milo panted but kept near me. Could I climb these too? I still would have the deadly claws to deal with. I yanked at the short strands of my hair and cursed. "Think, Misti, think."

Demon fight behind me, poisonous climb in front. I'll take door number three. I turned and tried to figure a way out. Wondering around by myself when the demon underworld were all after me didn't seem smart but I needed Paul and Axel.

If Axel had gotten himself killed I would be pissed. I groaned. "Alright, Milo. You and me."

Maybe I'd find Paul's friend. I ran back the way Paul went but kept a big space between me and the fight which was down to the lone demon and two of the beady eyed demon. The third lay on the ground in a mangled heap.

My shoulders bumped crates as the space got more and more narrow. I rushed past the one crate with busted wooden splinters on the ground. The other crates rattled and fear sent me through faster. The thought of facing dozens of crates containing demons did not appeal.

At the end of the passage I reached a small building. Looked like a small office pod but black out shades covered the windows. My breath hitched but I eased closer when I heard voices arguing inside.

"Where is she, Jericho? I swear if you—"

Axel?

My heart stuttered. Milo shot forward, tail high and barking in quick succession. The door swung open and Axel stepped out. Dirt dotted his shirt, a thin scratch marred his left temple and his black was hair disheveled but I'd never been so relieved to see someone.

"Axel, Paul ditched me again." My voice may have contained a whine mixed with the complaint. I didn't care.

"See? Unharmed as promised. Feel better?" The burly man standing in the doorway next to Axel wore an ankle leather duster the same color as the black hair slicked back from his face.

Axel marched toward me with a determined stride. His brows slashed across his forehead in a foreboding frown and his mouth dipped down at the corners. He grasped my jaw and tipped my face up. "Are you alright?"

This wasn't the Axel I was used to. My fun friend had left the building and in his place stood a very pissed demon whatever he was. The tone of his muttered question implied he was waiting for my answer to determine if there was ass in need of whipping.

I planted my hands on my hips and admitted, "I'm good but there are demons all over this place. If Paul's friend isn't here, we need to go."

Milo barked and ran circles around us. Axel dropped his hand and bumped my shoulder with a slight grin. "You're like a demon magnet."

That didn't make me feel better.

"You're alive, that's all that matters." The man shouted from the door.

"Speaking of being alive, what the hell, Axel? Where were you?"

"Calm down! I'm here now. I came back down and you were gone but then I ran into him." He pointed to the mystery man.

"Oh, so it's my fault?" yelled the man. "More like you all invaded my space, interrupting my private sanctuary. On top of that, she's the one all of Hell is searching for. Great!"

I looked to Axel but he merely shrugged.

"Well don't stand there. Both of you come in."

We entered the office and a human sized cage hung from the ceiling. Inside was an alabaster demon similar to the one that escaped from the crate and the others just another color.

"My prize has awakened."

Apparently, Axel knew what was going on when the man walked over and rattled the cage. I jumped back and Milo barked. Inside the pale creature huddled in the corner.

"Why is that thing here, in there? What are you going to do with it?"

"None of your concern. And my name is Jericho Scorcher."

Chapter 17

I decided I didn't like him. Not that it said much, considering every demon to cross our path so far wanted to kill me. Turning to Axel, I asked. "Is this Paul's friend? Can we get the book and go?"

Nothing about this guy made me want to be around him longer than necessary. Axel rubbed the back of his neck.

Jericho didn't seem to like me either and shot me a dark look. "Who are you to make demands around here? You two get out. I have work to do."

"Wait, she doesn't understand, Jericho. We've been through a lot. She's new to our world, Randall wanted to recruit her, Jason attacked her and things escalated from there."

"That was you?" Jericho eyed me in a new light. "No, there's no way in hell that was you. You're too small and thin to have taken down a Jason. Now don't get me wrong," he clarified when I frowned at him. "I didn't like the son-of-a-bitch. He was a thorn in my side and I'd be the first to congratulate you, but I just can't wrap my head around it."

I wondered if this meant he wouldn't help us.

Axel shifted slightly to block me from Jericho's sight. "We're here about the book containing the information on the demon hunters."

"Word travels fast in the underworld." Jericho exhaled and folded his arms across his chest. "Everyone under and on the surface is looking for Misti Calloway, the last descendant of the most powerful demon hunting family."

That didn't sound good to me. "Don't you want to collect the bounty too?"

"If I wanted to collect that bounty you would be in this cage instead of this low level demon. Lucky for you I'm not interested."

He turned his attention back to the cage. The creature inside gripped the bars and howled. It still quivered with fright and knowledge of its doomed fate. "Now, please leave."

"Gladly. Misti, let's get the hell outta here. I knew he was no help." Axel grabbed a hold of my arm, and pulled me back out the door.

"Wait, I don't understand." I anchored my feet on the floor, stopping Axel from pulling me further. "Are you the guy Paul insisted we meet? He said you could help."

"Paul shouldn't have brought you here," Jericho snapped, his face turning red.

Alright-y, mister nice guy. "Blame Paul but we need help on finding this book."

"Oh, I know damn well about all the chaos you've caused in the last few days," Jericho scoffed. "Everyone's out looking to collect your bounty for the big man himself."

Axel stiffened. "What else can you tell us? What does Randall have planned?"

I briefly wondered if Jericho would turn us into Randall despite his claim not to be interested in my bounty. Exactly how much was I worth?

"I don't want to get involved," Jericho enunciated, meeting our stares evenly.

Axel whipped out his lighter and began flipping the lid open and closed. Click, click. Click, click. Jericho's eyes latched onto it and for the first time I saw true fear glint there.

"For all time sakes, Jerry, why don't you tell us what we know and Misti and I will be on our way."

While Axel spoke calmly there was nothing calm about the look the two exchanged.

"Listen, Axel. We go way back. So I'm only going to tell you this and then I hope our paths don't cross any more." Jericho nodded his head in my direction. "Your little friend's presence on the scene has changed things. Every demon under the sun wants to end her with or without the bounty because of what she can do."

I gulped. Hell had to be a really bad place if even the demons didn't want to be there. "We're desperate at this point. We'll give you anything."

"Misti, don't promise him anything."

But it was too late. Jericho Scorcher named his price. He mouth curved into wicked grin. I already regretted not listening to Axel's initial offer to leave.

"The Hellhound. Give him to me." A blunt finger aimed Milo's way.

Jericho's demand caught me off guard. "You want my dog?"

"Yes. Hellhounds have a history of helping demon hunters during their hunts. That's why he's attached himself to you."

I found it hard to grasp the idea of my innocent puppy as a Hellhound. My visceral reaction to leaving Milo was immediate. "No, you can't have my dog."

"Fine. No deal then," he waved us off. "Leave!"

Unholy

I picked up Milo prepared to find another way.

"How long?" Axel interrupted my dramatic Axel.

I gave him crazy eyes. We were not leaving my dog with this maniac.

Jericho glanced from me to Milo curled in my arms and in now way resembled a Hellhound. "One week."

"No!"

"Agreed."

Axel and I spoke at the same time.

"Nothing happens to the hound while we're gone," my BFF added as if that made things better.

"Done." Jericho's eyes lit with greed as he came toward me and reached for Milo.

Much to my surprise he didn't snap or bite at Jericho. Who was this man?

Axel shifted to my side and rubbed my shoulder. I elbowed him sharply and wanted to crow at his pained grunt.

"You can have the Hellhound in exchange for information about the book, about Misti's lineage, and anything you know about Randall's plans."

Jericho held Milo by his middle and lifted him toward the cage. I jerked but Axel held me in place. The creature in the cage crawled to the other side with a whine. Jericho laughed. "It's a Shadow Crawler. Hellhounds are good for finding any demon no matter the classification. I'm going to have fun with my new friend."

Axel rolled his eyes. "Start talking.

"Fine." Jericho pouted. It was not a good look on him. "Randall wants her dead, no surprise there. She's the only thing standing in his way with regards to the gates he keeps opening to allow demons to cross over from Hell. He's hoping to find favor with the dark king and raise his status."

Axel snorted. "There's always a demon jockeying for a position with Hades. What about the book? Where can we find it?"

"Ah, the book. No idea where it is." Jericho simply stated and smiled.

My mouth dropped. Had this all been a waste? "But Paul said you could help us."

"I can."

In and out. In and out. My breathing mantra came in handy. I fetched the mysterious paper out of my back pocket, and waved it in front of him. "What can you tell us about these symbols?"

"Sounds like to me you've stumbled upon a Watchmen's cave." Jericho explained after I described to him how I found these same symbols in the underground dungeon.

"I don't know how the Hunters entered the cave but I'll take your word for it. I've only heard about them. Then you found this guy?" Jericho pointed to Milo.

I nodded.

"And was this before or after you charred Jason to ash?"

"After." I wanted to snatch Milo from him. Something about the way he cradled my pet unnerved me.

"The book," Axel prodded.

"I don't know about the book, but the Watchmen were demon hunters who maintained peace between

Earth and Hell. If a demon escaped Hell and caused trouble up above, the Watchmen had to catch them and either returned them to Hell or have them executed. Depends on what they did."

"So why do demons and others refer to them as Hunters, other than because of the obvious?" Axel asked.

"You have no idea what the obvious reason is do ya, Wentz?" Jericho laughed. "Watchmen don't hunt. They maintain peace and arrest. They only kill when absolutely necessary. They're referred to as Hunters because some tended to go rogue and hunt demons for sport. It's a part of their curse. You know the saying, 'with great power' and all that crap. That's why I never wanted to be a good guy."

I always knew I was cursed. Great. As if this ability to kill people and demons alike with a touch of my hand. Now I'm destined to go off the rails. Fantastic.

Axel slipped his lighter back into his pocket and directed me toward the door. "That's all we needed."

"Like shit." I lamented.

Jericho reached to Axel and the two whispered furiously. I ignored them for the most part.

Once outside, Axel tried to calm my obvious nerves. "Don't let that shit Scorcher filled your head with get to you. You're not cursed, Misti. It's a gift. Your family line helps hold the balance."

"Yeah," I gritted at him. "And how do you know that? What makes you think I won't go off the handle and hunt you down for the hell of it, Axel?"

"You won't," he said firmly. "We're gonna get that book and you're gonna be the best damn *Watchmen*

Hell's ever seen. You're not gonna let shit get pass you. I'll make sure of that."

I gave him a crooked smile. "That's the best pick me up BFF speech anyone's ever given me."

"No prob. What are familiars for?"

A demon joke. Funny.

"Come on, let's get outta here. It'll be dark soon."

His Cheshire grin lightened the mood for us both. Afterwards, he locked a protective arm around my neck, guiding me through the terminal.

Chapter 18

In the parking garage, Axel tossed a set of keys in the air. I couldn't believe we wouldn't have to find a way to travel on our own. "I convinced Jericho to lend us his ride. He also gave me a map to check places for the book with a church highlighted."

That explained the last minute speech. I followed along, still down about leaving Milo. Axel shouted when he finally found the car he was looking for.

"This? This is our ride?" It was way out of left field but shouldn't have surprised me. "Really, Axel, a Hearse?" Black or a really, really dark grey in the light when it needed a wash. And from the thick layer of dust, a wash was definitely in the near future.

"What's wrong with it?" He asked fiddling with the keys.

"Don't you see the irony in this?" I laughed. This was too comical. Laughter was the only thing I could muster. "We're going to a church in the middle of the evening in a Hearse to fight demons. I mean, who writes this crap?"

"Well, what were you expecting, a tricked-out Cadillac?" he joked as he climbed in and waited for me to shut my door.

"As if Jericho would trust either of you two with his precious Delilah." A chorus of screams and swears filled the front seat as we twisted our necks to see the back.

"What the hell, Paul? We're not all immortal." Axel swore at our missing companion.

I was pissed more than anything. Twice, Paul had left me. "Where the hell have you been?"

He had the audacity to joke. "Man, I thought I was bad. The worry-wart spirit is rubbing off on everyone now, huh?"

Axel spread the paper open on his lap. "Here's the map he drew out for us. He said the basilica would be our best bet for the book. No demon in their right mind would dare go onto holy ground and expect to come out in one piece. Then this." Jericho had drawn a zig-zag line with 'Wash. Mon.' labeled at the end.

"The Washington Monument?" I wondered. "But why?"

"Something about when it was originally built it was used as a sun dial and helped monitor the moon phases," Axel described.

"Of course. That makes complete sense." Paul signaled Axel to drive and he started muttering.

I stared at Paul through the rear view while he talked to himself. "Have something to share with the class, Paul. It's not nice to be selfish."

"So what do you think? Are his assumptions worth checking out or what?" Axel asked me.

I shrugged. "What other choice do we have? Every lead is worth checking out."

Axel pushed at my arm while he drove and I bumped into the door. "We're going to find the book and kick Randall's ass."

"Speaking of Randall."

Axel and I let out a chorus of yelps when Paul popped his head back up between us from the back. Paul rubbed his hands together like a psycho mastermind. "You're powerful. Once you learn your abilities, strengths and weaknesses you'll be unstoppable."

"Because I won't join him, he plans to kill me," I added.

Paul shrugged. "There's that too."

"Well, that's not gonna happen." The Hearse came to a sudden halted. I nearly crashed my head into the dashboard. "We're here."

Axel had parked us right in front. We all got out, although Paul more or less stumbled from the back, taking a casket with him to the ground.

"This is too much. Please, tell me Jericho, doesn't also moonlight as an undertaker?" I can't believe I still had it in me to be amused.

"I don't know what he does in his spare time." Paul's answer was blasé.

A group of clergymen congregated on the front steps of the church.

"What do you think is happening?" Neither replied to my question, instead staring at the men huddled together. Soon a hysterical woman crashed into their group screaming and clutching onto them desperately.

"Axel, look." Paul's eyes directed us to the setting sun, illuminating the horizon. They both peered back at one another and like a switch, they flipped from panic then instantly to battle ready mode.

"What's happening? Why are you two freaking out?"

The lid of the casket popped open to reveal a very large, odd shaped gun. Clearly a demon modified weapon since I'd never seen the likes. Axel grabbed it up, a look of pleasure crossing his face. "I'll need this. I'm glad Jericho likes to be prepared."

"Misti," Paul said hastily, "there's a reason why the paper only depicts three phases of the moon and not all of them. The waning period, full moon and wading period."

I groaned. "Let me guess, that's the one in the middle."

"Right," Paul and Axel said together.

"Paul, stay out here and keep watch." Axel turned to me. "Let's go."

"Are we expecting trouble here?" I stared in awe at the fact he wanted to bring a gun into a church. A big one. "You can't take that inside with us."

Axel hefted the gun higher, and used the strap to toss it over his shoulder. "First this isn't an ordinary gun. Second, this is potentially a gate site for demons. I'm not taking you in there without something to use as protection."

I held up my hand and focused hard. My gift stirred and my hand burned. I was getting better at this. "We have protection."

I didn't appreciate Paul's dismissive chuckle.

"Second," Axel continued, ignoring my mini-boast. "This beauty is loaded with a special serum that would put your powers to shame. Jericho catches his prey that he tracks because he uses the best weapons. As you're familiar, I'm obligated to do everything possible to make sure you don't die."

"Alright, alright. I'll help too," Paul chimed in. He stepped next to me and lifted up his shirt.

I flinched at the unsightly bulges. "Easy there."

Paul withdrew a knife the length of my forearm. "You might need this."

"Right, here's the plan. I'll find another way inside. Both of us going in might draw suspicion. You see the dome there?" Axel pointed to the structure. "At the sun's height, it shines directly above the glass, same for the moon."

"Impressive."

Axel smirked. "Get inside and search the dome area. That's our best bet. IF you sense demon activity get out."

I agreed. He nudged my shoulder one last time and darted off to the right. I waited until his figure disappeared around the side of the building. I could do this. No demons were getting the best of me. I crossed my fingers.

Chapter 19

There was no issue getting inside. I received a few glances, some followed by a smile of acknowledgment. All those eyes on me would normally freak me out but after the last few days, the fact that they were human outweighed any concerns. I sat in a center bench several rows back from the pulpit.

The majority of the congregation huddled under the candlelight vigil on their knees in the floor. I was mystified by the fiery candles dancing on top of the partially darkened pulpit. I tried ignoring its hypnotic spell over me but the flames beckoned me to come closer. In the event of not drawing any unnecessary attention to myself, I thought it would be best to follow their lead and join them in the front. I mimicked the others and lifted a burning candle to relight another dwindling one by its side.

"Be still, my child. Everything will be fine on the other side. Believe in him and he will welcome you with open arms."

I lifted my head up to the nun patting me on the shoulder. When she gave me a pale yellow handkerchief, I realized I was crying. Gratefully, I accepted her offer, and wiped away my treacherous tears.

"Why don't you tell me what has you worried, my child? You are safe here." Her voice was soft and calming despite all the chaos brewing within and outside the clean and bright white walls.

Another nun attempted to enter behind a violet curtain but was stopped by a strange guy. Dressed in all black, he guarded the corner adjacent to both the curtain and a closed wooden door.

"I'm fine, Sister, thanks." Did you still call nuns sister? I went with it since it seemed appropriate and decided to lie a bit. "I'm struggling to stay afloat with my life right now. As you can see, I don't have much to speak of. I can't find steady work or food to eat."

"Not to worry, my child. He knows your pain and all will be soothed in the afterlife. With time all will be right again." She sounded like she was reading from a script.

"Excuse me, my child. Others need my assistance at the moment as well." She nodded and glided away.

I needed something to distract the man from his corner to peek inside that door and pass the curtain. Only a little bit of time remained for me to rejoin Axel and Paul and I had nothing worked out yet.

I glanced over to the sounds of moaning where the nun was now placating a hysterical woman. The nun was hushing her, which only drew more nosey glances, murmurs, and stares. Then, the woman saw me and instantly became silent. Her mouth and eyes wide open, she lifted her hand and pointed it straight at me.

She was dressed in clothes that had seen better days. Not shabby but not couture, a simple pair of pants that probably had an elastic waist and a pullover top. She walked towards me, stomping heavily in a pair of battered boots. I stepped back when she almost reached me.

"You . . . you . . ." She whispered.

The nun placed a soft, wrinkled hand on her shoulder to pull her back only to be easily shaken off.

"You are who they want . . .you will kill us all!"

"What? No, I don't know what you're talking about." I turned, only to see the frowning, stone-faced man in the corner.

I kept retreating and then stopped maybe three feet from the lone guard. I allowed her to get within a little more than an arm's reach of me before she finally got a handful of my shirt.

"You are marked with the curse! The Hell's minions are searching for you and will not stop until they find you!" she hissed.

How the hell does she know that? Is she a demon too?

I tried to loosen her grip from me but I didn't think I could have even if I didn't want her too. This woman was playing the role better than I could have imagined.

"What do you want from me? What's happening?" I played my part with the shaky voice and eventual hot tears wetting my cheeks.

"Miss, leave this poor girl be. No need to take your fears and concerns out on her. We all feel the presence of the devil in us but you mustn't let him win," the nun pleaded.

The woman wasn't listening. I pushed myself further back. Large, strong hands pressed into my back holding us into place in front of the guard. The woman continued pushing me even with the man stopping us both from going any further to the door. They struggled with me in between trying to escape the woman's clutches, and get past the guard without causing too much suspicion.

Unholy

We were drawing more attention. While others joined in and scuffled on the floor, I made my escape. Chaos was erupting when I rejoined the congregation. Blasts violently shook the building, blowing holes in the marble. Men, women, and children all both young and elderly hollered for a savior. Many huddled by the candlelight, cementing their entry into their desired afterlife. Suddenly, the doors blasted opened completely destroying the door and throwing everyone back several feet.

I search around for what was causing all this destruction but nothing ever entered passed the church hall's threshold other than balls of fire.

Demons.

I had to get out of here and rejoin the others. The guard was nowhere to be found, his corner abandoned. Pulling the thick, velvety curtain aside, I ran down a narrow hallway that led another similar looking stairwell. I'm convinced the same architect designed both the church and the underground dungeon. This stairwell was just as long, I couldn't get down the damn thing fast enough. Finally to the bottom, I was met with another long, brick-layered tunnel.

"Misti, down here hurry!" Axel called out to me when I finally saw him sliding out from behind some other wall further down.

I raced to him freaked the hell out as he aimed his gun in front of him. Then, he dove onto the other side of the same wall, forcing me to stop in my tracks from the exchange of weapon fire.

"What's going on down here?" I yelled through the gun blasts and pressed against his back.

"What's going on down *here*? What's going on up *there*?" He fired his gun back through the hall and then spoke again. "I was waiting for you down here but the next thing I know the building started shaking. I had half a mind to come up there and get you myself."

We ducked and dodged more blasts aimed our way. Axel continued explaining the situation in between returning fire.

"Then out of nowhere this hole was blasted through the wall. Good thing neither of us were down this way when it hit. But when I ran down here to see everything exploded around me. I ducked back down this way and then saw you. Stay close to me, Misti."

"Some lady actually attacked me. She knew about the hunters."

Axel cursed. "We need to get you out of here. Too many demons and this feels like a set-up but I don't know how."

Debris fell everywhere and dust filled the air between us. When Axel returned fire, I hopped around him to the adjacent wall, behind his line of fire.

If we left we'd never know if the book was here. I needed it to learn about my family line and to defeat Randall. "I'll go find this damn book and come back. Just don't leave me."

Indecision crossed his face but he finally nodded. "You've got 5 minutes."

I sprinted further down the tunnel into a large room under one of the domes. I searched along the doorframe and eventually found it. The moon phases symbol. They matched exactly.

"This has to be it."

Unholy

I pulled out my borrowed knife, and frantically dug into the wall. The hole expanded on either side when something finally plopped out.

If I didn't know any better I would've left it thinking it was just another muddy brick or solid piece of clay that didn't crumple to bits. I wiped the dried clay and dirt from a brown leather-bound book, the size of my palm. The cover was surprisingly plain and in pristine condition even after hundreds of years down here.

Siked, I stuffed the book in the back of my jeans and prepared myself for the hell we had to go through to escape those demons that were attacking us. I crept back into the tunnel with my hunting knife ready by my side. All was quiet. I didn't take that as a good sign.

"Go! I'm right behind you," Axel yelled.

I listened for once without arguing and made my way back. I burst through the side door of the church, others running behind me in a panic. Sirens sounded in the distance.

"Misti, oh thank heavens." Paul almost crashed into me, running from the opposite direction. I sagged in relief, putting away my knife. "Axel. Where's Axel?"

"At the car."

Paul and I trotted to the hearse.

"He was like this when I came this way looking for him." Paul bounced on his heels.

That was when I saw him. "What happened?"

Axel lay sprawled on his back, the gun gripped in his lax hand. My heart froze and my throat locked. I checked for a pulse, sighing in relief when I found one. It was faint, but it was there. Paul rambled on about wanting to help but was too late after Axel dispatched the demons who'd chased him outside.

"We have what we need. Help me with him and let's get out of here."

Paul did what he could but ultimately left me with lifting Axel up by myself. As he cleared the way ahead of us, I noticed blood on the back of his buzzed head.

"Damn it!" I hissed. Axel didn't just fall and hit his head. My jaw tensed. "He better not have done what I think he did." I whispered into Axel's ears, and moaned barely audible.

"Let me help." Paul and I each grabbed an arm and managed to get Axel in the back seat, stretched across the leather.

I eased the strap of the gun from his shoulder and placed it on the floor.

"Now I see the irony in all of this," Paul chuckled. He stopped when I shot him a hard stare.

"Come on, get in."

"It's better to walk from here. The Monument's literally blocks from here, two down and two across. They won't be expecting it. Plus, it gives us time for a plan and I can explain the book to you," he advised.

I double-checked Axel's pulse while I considered Paul's suggestion. Every ounce of sense in my mind screamed 'Don't you dare go on your own with this loser! Remember last time!' but what choice did I have? An inch closer to foiling Randall's plans was better than running away any day.

"Come on, he'll be fine. He just needs his rest before he's up to fighting shape again." Paul said as he placed a reassuring hand on my shoulder.

I made sure Axel was comfortable, and closed the back door.

One of those demons tried to kill us. They almost succeeded with Axel. Randall would pay.

I needed to get my demon banishing ju-ju to work on time tonight. No false charges. I squeezed my hands as hard multiple times when I remembered the memory of Axel out cold.

Paul and I started for the monument, briskly walking side by side. I didn't trust him and kept my guard up. "What should we do?"

"We go find out what Randall is planning for tonight, stop him therefore delaying any other future plans, and maybe take out one or two of his minions."

"So no plan," I deadpanned. Great, just great.

"Well, I don't hear you coming up with anything, demon hunter. This is your domain."

Shit. He was right. For once.

"Here," I slammed the book into his gut. "Search through there and find anything on how to banish multiple demons. No doubt Randall will have his gang waiting. Anything useful. I'll keep watch." I was stuck with the dope, didn't mean I had to put my life in his hands. Again.

Paul hungrily crammed his head inside the small journal. Then, I heard noise creeping up from down the road behind us.

"Stop," I ordered Paul.

"What is it? What do you hear?"

The roaring stopped and I thought I was hearing things. Slowly, I dropped my arm from Paul's, and we continued hiking. But only after a few steps did the roaring start back up again, this time louder. Lights shined down the street at the light we just past, gaining speed with an insane, blinding brightness. Paul and I ducked into nearby bushes and watched as the unknown assailant drove pass us.

"Come out, Calloway. We know you're out here. Don't make us come and get ya', now." I saw one person I was sure to be a demon sent by Randall to collect me, riding on an ATV roaring on the street. They revved their engines to taunt me out of hiding. Paul and I froze, holding our breaths. Even shallow breathing was out of the question in fear these demons may have super hearing.

"Aw, don't want to play, aye? Suit ya'self."
The Brit from back at the shop.

He roared his engine twice more before he revved and turned back down the road. We sprinted in his direction until we reached the bottom of the hill, and hid against the adjacent street corner to scope out the scene. There was who I presumed to be another demon patrolling, walking back and forth along the street near where we hid. I signaled we split up and Paul agreed before the demon turned back around. When he strolled to the other side, I quickly vaulted over and hid in between one of the lawn's stone barricades and brightly colored bushes.

Paul hid behind some cars going up the hill. I contemplated running for the stairs next to another barricade higher up but a better idea came to me when the patroller turned back around, walking in my direction again. I concentrated on the last week. I needed everything I suppressed deep down in my gut to boil back to the surface if I wanted my revenge on Randall for what he put me through. Kidnapping me then blowing up my home, forcing me to face a demonic spider, allowing an intentional attack on me in the library, sending a bounty out of me and Axel, the Shadow Crawlers. Now Axel being out for the count.

I was sure they all possessed something that made them useful to Randall or he wouldn't have released them from Hell. So I wasn't exactly surprised when I could clearly hear the demon sniffing in the night air for my scent more than likely. I palmed the knife and braced myself between the small pillars in the barricade.

"Come out, girlie," he ordered.

"Should I?" I thought. "I can't hide here forever." I swirled the idea around in my head for a few seconds before I heard the cock of his gun shockingly close to my hiding spot.

Determination and numbness took over as fear crippled me. I had no issue popping back out from my hiding spot and vaulting over the stone hurdle to him. His weapon aimed at me, he then laughed at my appearance.

I faced him, knowing I was a sight. Filthy face covered in dirt and grime, holding a knife the length of my forearm that I had no clue how to wield and in way over my head with this demon crap. Yeah, I was a joke. A joke to him and everyone else I'd encountered so far, and after every one of those encounters, I've proven them wrong. This time, hopefully, would be no different.

"Well, howdy pretty lady. What an honor to finally meet you." He bowed theatrically.

The southern one Sam hit at the shop.

"What do you want with me?"

"What, no howdy back? That's mighty rude of ya' darlin'. Lucky for you, I'm a forgiving man. Now why don't you come with me like a good girl? I don't want to have to hurt you now."

He lowered his weapon, and quickly grabbed my wrist like he was afraid I would try to pull and run away. But run where, right into another demon that would probably shoot and sedate me on sight to claim his prize. The look on his face when I didn't pull away was almost as sweet as it was pathetic. First, shock that I even let him touch me let alone grab a handful of my arm. Then, a smirk crept up his face into a shameless toothy grin excluding several front teeth.

I guess new teeth weren't a part of the benefits package when working with Randall.

"So what do you plan to do to me if your friends don't get a hold of me first?" I asked. He stopped pulling and halted altogether before he turned and frowned at me.

"They don't get you. I do. I turn you over to Randall and I get you back in return for my loyalty to him."

"Is that what he promised you? What else did he say to make you swear allegiance to him? Did he add in your own kingdom, riches and gold, and other women you couldn't pull even during your mortal life?" He ignored me, and resumed tugging me along to the others. I saw light up at the top of the hill closer to the bottom of the monument and figured they were all up there, waiting for Randall to eventually show. Suddenly, a voice cracked from his side; a walkie-talkie. Another army knife was attached to his thigh.

"Virgil, get back on our post."

"How long do you think you'll get to have me before your friends take me away from you and claim me as their own? Just one more thing you'll have to share with them." I forced the vomit-inducing question, tugging a bit for his attention before he could reach for the radio.

"Randall promised . . . They're my brothers; they wouldn't do that to me." The radio squawked again while I continued taunting him.

"The same brothers who pick on you I bet. Who make you go last or get last pick? Tell me *Virgil*, what humiliating things did they make you do before they let you join their little gang to get out of Hell? Were they bad, I mean, really, really bad?"

"You don't know anything." He yanked me to him until I could tell he hadn't brushed his teeth in possibly a decade or however long he had been dead. "On your knees," he commanded.

"What?"

"I said, On. Your. Knees." He squeezed my wrist even tighter to emphasize every word. I thought he would break it. Maybe he did have a backbone after all.

Chapter 20

"You wanna know how I winded up in Hell, little missy? The things I had to do?" He reached precisely for the sweet spot between my wrist and forearm and twisted it back at a painful angle to ensure I sunk to my knees as he ordered.

From the glee on his monstrous face, he loved my contorted features but it got him off even more that I couldn't scream. I tried absorbing the pain, I wouldn't dare alert the others of my torment so they could join in too. I had to figure a way to survive and last until Axel regained conscious.

At last, Virgil let my wrist free. I cradled my hand, he looked around before he lifted and aimed his gun back up at me. His radio squawked for a third time and for a third time, he didn't answer. If anything, he turned it down to almost silent.

"If they do take you from me, I want to say I already had my turn with you."

Oh God! Is this how he got into Hell?

I hid my face from him but I didn't miss the hand still aiming the gun at me while the other slowly slid down his pants leg and onto his crouch, gripping himself. He nudged the gun at my forehead, forcing me to look up at him. His rotten, toothy grin made another disgusting appearance while his calloused fingers glided down his zipper. It was either the rotten teeth or the genitals, if his mouth was any indication to his personal hygiene and overall appearance, the grin won out.

Unholy

I gasped pretending to see something behind him, and his attention followed. Without thinking it through, I head-butted his partially zipped pants. He fired a round into the air, alerting the others now. Back on my feet, I kicked his gun out of his hands, straddled him, and pressed my grimy hands firmly against his face.

My power soared up. His face began to burn, steam smoking from his melting flesh. He attempted to push me off. Back and forth we struggled but he was no match against my Hunter line. I loved that name. Totally better than Watchmen.

Virgil struggled to speak, to scream, to even blink and swallow. "Don't send me back," he croaked.

I winked. "Buh, bye."

His body folded in on itself just like Jason and Virgil was no more.

I wiped my hands on my pants pocket and kept the extra knife. I paused at the sound of soft whispers by Virgil's death spot. I spun around at the scorched ground where he'd lain. There was no way he could've survived that attack. Unless he was like Paul—please God don't let it be true. If so then killing Virgil was just a waste of time.

Then, I remembered the radio. Picking it up, I turned the knob only a little to hear murmurs of someone coming to see where Virgil was. The sun had long since set. Using the waning light to my advantage, I ducked in and out of the foliage. I cut diagonally across the lawn when I heard someone running down the sidewalk in my direction.

Finally, at the next barricade, I heard hushed voices discussing my whereabouts. I even heard Axel's name a few times. I really wished he was here. But then I thought, Fuck that! You're doing a pretty bitchin' job killing demons. Did you not see your own handy work, Calloway?

I relaxed. Not as good as Axel's pick up speech but it worked and I felt renewed confidence. After scolding me for leaving him and trusting Paul, Axel would have totally said that. I wondered how he was doing. Was he up and wondering where Paul and I were. If so I hoped was on his way here now despite feeling like I was doing well on my own. I peered back down the hill, abruptly killing that dream when I saw the same guy that passed me on my way up kneel beside the burned circle where Virgil had made his return trip to hell. My stolen radio relayed the same words he said into his albeit with a delayed echo. I turned it silent and went to ditch it when a holler called out over the lawn.

"Find her!" Footsteps scattered above me, disappearing into the midnight darkness.

One at the bottom and the other two abandoned their posts.

Swiftly, I ran up what was left of the steep hill to find Paul rummaging through the book's pages. I called for his attention but either completely unaware or unsurprised of my presence, Paul never lifted his head up from the book. I quickly ran towards him and tried snatching the book from him. He hastily pulled it back.

"You don't understand," he rushed completely exasperated. "This is bigger than you and I. I have been waiting for this moment for what feels like an eternity, and I can't . . . I won't let you stop me."

Unholy

"Paul what are you talking about?" I asked in a hushed voice. Then it dawned on me. "You better not be telling me what I think you are, Paul. Don't do this. You aren't that guy. You don't have it in you."

But he was. And he did.

He appeared to relent and lowered the book from his sight for the first time since I appeared in front of him. Paul was my friend. Kinda. I depended on him for information in all of this madness. Even if he was a selfish asshole—and that didn't even begin to cover the amount of obscenities to describe him.

Paul moved to speak but then, without a moment's notice, all the spotlights on each corner exploded, instead, three spotlights shined insanely bright in front of the monument's iron barricade in front of Paul and I.

We stumbled back from the blinding lights until they dimmed down by half. Soon after, the most nerve-wracking sound assault my ears and the foulest smelling fog seeped from the monument. Like the tomb the statue itself stood upon was coming alive like an Egyptian emperor awaking after being buried alive after millennia. And he smelled like one too.

Foolishly, I let my guard down too long, focusing on Paul and then the tomb. I never caught notice of the men who surrounded us and took a bullet in the back of my knee. Before gravity even had a chance to pull me down, I was yanked back up again onto my knees.

I'd never been shot. Excruciating pain burned up my leg.

"Ey there, luv? Don't squirm, you'll just make it worse."

The Brit. That leaves the South African and the . . .

Sam—the Australian—casually strolled in front of me. "You are one elusive Sheila, Misti Calloway." He announced, twirling a toothpick between his lips. He was the most polished of the pack from this angle. Of course, jeans and cowboy boots were quintessential for life in the outback. But 'Sheila'? How old was this guy? Did they still say that down there?

"Please excuse my brother's use of force but, when we saw what you did to poor Virgil, we couldn't take any chances, now could we?" He paced back and forth in front of us oh so nonchalant while I was bleeding out.

"You were in the shop when we arrived weren't you, Calloway? You and that familiar of yours. Where's the coward anyway?"

"I should have put it together. I should have known better. As long as they're protecting their companion, they can hide in plain sight. That's why I could smell them but couldn't spot them in the store."

The African's complaint filled my head as I grew dizzy. How did people in the movies get up and jump tall buildings after being shot? That shit was a lie. I could barely keep my head up and wanted to curl on the ground.

"Do not fret, brother. He fooled us all, but not our friend Paul here. Cowards of a feather, flock together, don't they, Paul?"

I didn't hear anything from Paul but then again, I was struggling with consciousness and water filled my ears. I attempted to escape every time the Brit loosened his grip on my collar. Growing frustrated with my lack of stability, he twisted my aching arm back while tightening his grip on my collar, practically choking me.

I wish you would make up your mind. Do you want me to bleed out or suffocate me to death? Pick one, not both.

"Not talking, Paul? Not attempting to snake your way out of this one? Well, our friend here may have something to say about that." Sam immediately stepped aside as if on cue to the introduction of none other than Randall Clark.

Why are you doing this, Paul? What has Randall promised you? Nothing will change who you are.

"Ah, here we all are. Together at last!" He announced exuberantly. Standing firm and taller than ever, his shiny blonde mane neatly tied behind him, not one golden strand out of place. His maroon three-piece suit transitioned from a dark to a bright red gradient in the many spotlights under him, giving the illusion of blood; how fitting.

"My dear, Misti Calloway, how nice it is to see you again!" I could hear the glee in his fake greeting. He reached to pull my head back up and looked me in the eyes until I stilled my head to his attention.

"There we are. We don't want you leaving us just yet, now do we?" He snapped his fingers and all but an ache lingered in my leg. The relief was only temporary when rope was wrapped around my wrists and I was knocked to the ground with a swift blow to the back of my head.

"Careful, Gary, my boy. How can you enjoy your prize when it's dead?"

"Sorry, Mr. Clark." The Brit named Gary apologized sheepishly. However, the scolding didn't stop Gary from holding me still on my stomach by pressing a firm boot into the back of my thighs.

"We're all here, Mr. Clark. At sunset during the Full Moon, just like you asked." Sam divulged to his master, not looking so much like the leader he portrayed himself to be only seconds ago.

"What, no boss man? No aye, aye, sir? What happened to calling the shots mate?" I mocked at Sam.

"Watch your tongue bitch!" the African hissed and a strong stomp was added by Gary in defense for their gang leader. At least I found a chink in the second in command. I had to get rid of the brute named Gary before I could ever get to those two.

"Now, now, gentlemen. Let's all calm down. Let our, Miss Calloway, have her pathetic and desperate attempt at grasping straws, still hiding behind her foolish denial. For after tonight, she will choose her fate in regards to her abilities. If not, she will no longer serve any purpose other than your plaything to pass around when I'm done with her."

"You asshole, Randall, what do you want from me?"

"It doesn't matter anymore, now does it luv? Now up you go," Gary instructed as he pulled me up by my tight bounds.

"Now, I will give you one last chance. But if I can't convince you, my lieutenants will. Allow me to provide an incentive to sway your decision." The African stepped back, casually walked behind Gary and me, and another blinding spotlight shined at the head of the monument. I noticed no one else craned their necks in awe and sheer horror at what hung at the top.

"You bastard!" Axel's back was strapped on the tip of the monument with his legs dangling freely in the air. The fact that he still floated on its top without falling down several stories was a sheer miracle. He had to have been conscious to maintain such balance at that height.

"Now that I have your full attention, what shall it be, Miss Calloway?"

"Please Randall, let him down. It's me you want, not him," I cried.

"Aww, a pair of lovebirds we have on our ands' aye, fellas?" The three men joined in on the laughter that only grew stronger when Gary loosened his hold on me, letting me fall back to my knees.

"Let him down, Randall. This wasn't a part of the deal. He was only protecting his companion. That's what they do."

Finally, Paul chimed in, and the laughter died down. Through my tears, I saw Paul offer me a sympathetic glance. Randall snapped his fingers and before I knew it Axel's limp body had floated and was placed in front of me.

"Wake him up," I growled.

"That's not how this works dear. I give you what you want and then you give me what I want. It's called an exchange of services. I've fulfilled my part of the bargain, now it's your turn." Axel's body didn't look as if they'd added to his injuries.

His breathing was shallow but I didn't know how long they had him up there teetering with death. He had come to my aid so many times within the past week, risking his life trying to give me a little bit more time for a stronger chance against Randall. I didn't want it to be in vain but, to come this far only for him to be gone before it was over seemed to be too much of a disservice to everything we've endured and too much to bear.

"I'll do it."

"Solomon, if you will?" The African named Solomon, returned from behind Gary and me and pulled a switch blade out of his pocket, handing it to Randall.

"Young Gary, remove that filthy leather from her. It's an eye sore." Gary proceeded as told by tearing the fabric as barbarically as possible using an already torn hole in my sole treasured possession.

"What of these other bits, Mr. Clark?" He asked a little too enthusiastically.

"Did I say strip her of her clothes or just the jacket, boy?" Randall responded fiercely. I could feel Gary retreat back but then mumbled swear words after the scolding. I thought Virgil was sensitive, but this Gary was incredibly both sensitive and irritable at being told what to do.

"I'm a grown man being scolded like a chil'. Who the hell does 'e think 'e is?" He whispered.

"The man who just magically cured me of my excruciating pain and the same who floated a body from atop a twelve-story statue." I rebutted. He growled in my ear and then, shoved me forward.

"Now let's remove these restraints, shall we?" And with another snap of his fingers, the rope loosened and fell off my wrists.

Unholy

"Now down to business," Randall announced. "I've asked you all here under this glorious Full Moon for an opportunity to join me in my quest for ultimate domination of both Hell and Earth. One variable has been dealt with, onto the other." He glanced back at me then, continued his spiel.

"Miss Calloway, you ask why you? But, did you ever think why not? The tingling sensation you felt when you came within an arm's reach of someone not from this realm, that wasn't a coincidence. You are the last addition I have been searching for to add to my court in the rise of my new kingdom."

"And what exactly will I be doing, Randall?" I asked feeling foolish I dropped my hand.

"Lift up your hand where I can see it. You have not fulfilled your part of the bargain yet," he demanded. Stubbornly, I lifted my hand back up in front of me in plain view of everyone.

"See, it's here. Now can you get on with it and tell me what I have to do with all of this?"

"Are ya' sure this is the person you've been searching for, Mr. Clark? She's a bit of a jester, ain't she? Doesn't know when to keep her mouth shut." Solomon added.

"She's got spunk, I like it." Gary winked.

"I chose you didn't I, Solomon? And you too Samuel, Gary? Do you not trust my decisions thus far? Should I be questioning your allegiance to me?" Randall's tone began to harden and rise at thought of his lieutenants betrayal.

"No, Mr. Clark. Solomon didn't mean it like that. He was curious is all. Ain't that right, Solomon?" Solomon nodded at both Samuel and Randall.

"Curiosity killed the cat, don't you know Solomon? Keep your questions to yourself if you choose to survive. Remember who released you all and gave you this glorious opportunity to serve by me."

"Now for your role in all of this, dear." Randall returned his unwanted attention back to me. "As a demon hunter by nature, because that's what you are which I'm sure you've figured out by now, I am in need of a mortal keeper here on earth."

"So a babysitter?" I spat. "All this so I could watch over your precious demons you can't be bothered with. All while you take over the world. Is that right?" I laughed. "Like you said, I'm just a lonely cleaning lady. I'm nothing. What use could I really have for you?"

"This is your chance, dear. Isn't this what you wanted; a chance to prove yourself? Possibly more riches and glory than you could ever imagine. I can also offer you and your familiar protection for when the world is mine, you will both be safe. Who would be foolish enough to pass that up?"

"Okay, first of all, all that 'chance' crap I meant like a clean record or like a chance to go to school; to show I wasn't a fuck up, not demon hunting. And what does Axel have to do with this?"

"Don't play dumb, girlie, it's obvious 'e belongs to ya'," Gary chimed in.

Bad mistake. Randall swiftly swiped the air, making a clawing gesture towards him. A shriek bellowed from him, I twisted around to see Gary

153

looking down at his hand covered in blood dripping from his face. Four deep gashes were dragged across his face, including one of his eyes.

"If you won't get your men in line, then I will," Randall hissed at Sam. Both he and Solomon stood glued to their posts not caring to help Gary. Rage creased his brow and darkened his eyes; Virgil wasn't the only one they treated like shit and got the table scraps.

"You have a gift, Misti. A gift that hasn't been seen in generations. Do you think those events, those people you 'ran into' happened for no reason? They just were tests I carefully set in place for you; the morgue, the lady in the library full of useless information, the brute at the convenience store, the cemetery, Scorcher and all with the help from our dear friend Paul here?"

Paul lowered his head at the mention of his name, too ashamed to take the glory he so strived for.

"Don't be bashful, old friend. You shall claim your prize as well for your dutiful service. Let us begin our journey, shall we?" He flicked open the switchblade and without flinching sliced his hand open.

"We're swapping blood? No, that's gross. I don't know what you have. Isn't there another way to pledge my allegiance to you?"

"Gentlemen," Randall called out to the others. One by one, they all revealed individual healed slices of their allegiance the middle of their hands too.

"Do you really think you can get away with this Randall? How powerful can you really be if you need me on your side?" I taunted. That struck a chord.

He inched closer then, he leaned in closer where his dark eyes granted me access into a bottomless black pit of sorrow. Souls screamed for freedom, a taste for blood and chaos. Then suddenly, took one giant leap backwards. I closed my eyes tight for a moment to regroup.

Stand firm, don't let him overwhelm you. He feeds off your struggles and pain.

"Now that we have that squared away," he turned and handed the blade to me. "Your turn." With shaky hands, I took the blade from Randall, and turned the blade to the inside of my hand. The silver beamed in the moonlight, arrogantly showing off its sharpness and precision. I pressed the blade into my hand but stopped dead short of slicing.

"Wake him up first." I motioned to Axel's unconscious body. "There's no way I'm going through with this until I know he's okay," I insisted.

He frowned and rolled his eyes at my demand but, when Randall saw the blade remained in my palm, he snapped his fingers. Axel's eyes shot open, he took a deep gasp of air, his chest rising like he'd been resurrected.

Axel continued coughing violently while my thoughts tried to formulate a plan. He sat up in the center of a somewhat circle we all formed around him. He definitely didn't miss the guns pointed on him by the three men.

"So what did I miss?"

"Oh nothing, dear boy, you're just in time to see a king be crowned upon his throne." Randall returned his sight back to me then. "Misti, we had a deal; him for your blood."

"Misti, don't you do it! Don't you know what he's planning? He's going to use you like he's done with the rest of us. Don't do it, Misti." Axel tried getting to his feet but was met with a hard whip by Solomon's gun.

What do I do? Randall obviously can't be trusted, but how do I get out of this?

Axel's glassy eyes glazed back up at me, blood dripping from his mouth. I needed a diversion. I glanced over to Paul was but he was gone from sight.

"I've had enough of this. I'll do it myself," Gary sputtered as he came marching towards me and grabbed a hold of both my arms from behind. I heard Axel try to get up and help me again. The other two were quickly on him, holding him down. Gary's blood smeared all over my face and neck as he gripped my arms tightly, forcing my body to fit into his.

"Stop stalling, I will have my prize." He licked an open spot under my chin and slipped his hands further down my arms. I struggled to get away from him initially but, when I saw where his hands were traveling to, I only squirmed a little to make it appear I was putting up a fight. As soon as his sweaty palms reached my fists, he reeled back screaming in pain.

I elbowed him and gunned down the hill. Axel fought his way through the other two. I didn't see what happened to him—if they killed him or not but I did hear glass shatter, and the lawn became pitch black. My hiding spot was my own until I heard rummaging on the other side of me. I didn't dare call out for Axel. But the next thing I knew, a hand clasped my mouth shut. A knife in my back and a strong British accent confirmed my suspicions.

"I will claim my prize one way or ano'ver." He hushed me, and I could feel my shirt ripping as the knife moved up my back. A car exploded several feet from us, lighting up our hiding spot, and allowed me to see again if only briefly. I didn't know what to do then. I could've felt for his flesh again. I couldn't risk the commotion with the knife in such close proximity of my precious spine.

"Ol' Randall wants blood, I'll give it to him on a silver platter once we're done luv." He whispered into the back of my ear, licking its outer shell. I shuddered from the thought of being with him. Virgil wasn't any better but he was a step up from this maniac. After its snail pace, the blade finally reached my bra but halted when we both heard shuffling by our brushes.

Then, a whistle followed that made Gary grunt and distracted.

"What now?" He moaned. I felt him turn and the blade turned with him, still uncomfortably close to said spine. When nothing happened he returned his attention me but before he could do anything, there was a second whistle, similar to the last, and Gary lifted the knife from my back.

"Sounds like your little 'companion' is down for the count." He chuckled and told me to stay put. My relief faded, now replaced by that familiar anxiety and immense fear of a 'holy shit, what now?' kind of feeling.

That was too easy. He can't be gone. He could shoot me in the back.

That shuffling sound returned to my brushes and I decided right to make my move down the hill.

Disorient him, get him on his butt then run.

I stilled and waited for Gary's return, lifted up my foot to approximately face level, and when he popped back in to finish what he started, I'd pop his head right back out clean off his neck. Or at least try to. After a moment or two, that was exactly what happened, exactly as I planned, but it wasn't Gary's neck that snapped back.

A 'crunch' and a, 'dammit, Misti!' awoke me from my stealth mode back to reality at who I just kicked square in the face.

"Oh, Axel I'm sorry. I thought it was—"

"I know who you thought it was!" He sounded nasally and was probably squeezing the bridge of his nose to make that but it was pitch black. I could only try and feel to see if it was broken but, we both knew it was.

"Here, let me help put it back in."

"No, you'll make it worse!" He pulled back, returning a shove in my face now, thankfully with his hand. "Let's get out of here. Follow closely behind."

We ducked and ran for cover foot by foot back down the hill. We paused at the sight of fiery explosions happening simultaneously around us.

"Look," I pointed in one of the blasts direction for Axel. "Up there." Mid-way up the hill, Randall and two others were quickly marching towards something.

"Where's Gary?"

"Handled." Axel said pointedly. Enough for me.

Only one bright spotlight remained in order for me to get a decent look of the crowd. It was Paul, on his hands and knees, panting like a tired, old dog. Solomon kicked him over onto his back, followed up by Randall kneeling down to him, muddling up his really nice suit. Randall began searching for himself through Paul's clothes for something, presumably the book. Fortunately for us, Randall found nothing. Paul not so much.

Randall's sun kissed tresses flung loose from their neatly placed hair tie, flying wild and hitting Paul and the others in the process. Then he pulled Paul close to him, and stared into his eyes. Any other time I would've been upset by not being able to see the action, but from the sound of Paul's blood curdling screams, it made me grateful I couldn't.

"What's Randall doing? Does he have telepathy?"

Axel hushed me. Eventually, Randall composed himself in front of his lieutenants, stood, wiped his hands on his pants, spoke back down to Paul, and casually walked off back up to the top of the hill. Sam and Solomon, once clear of Randall's fury, both knelt down to Paul's panting body and searched him just as frantically as Randall. Again, nothing.

"Does he not have the book anymore? I don't understand."

Axel nudged me quiet as the scene continued to unfold. They both returned to their feet and started pacing. Something caught their attention back at the bottom of the monument, at the very top of the hill, and Sam was the first to tread up towards it.

"They're going back with Randall," Axel whispered. A genius didn't have to know where to.

Solomon remained by Paul and glanced up on the monuments' lawn for us before he was called back up the hill too.

It wasn't until Axel pulled at my holey shirt to say that it was clear to go to Paul now. We trekked back up the steep hill. Axel stayed a back a little, but I dropped to my knees beside Paul.

"What have you done? What did you do with the book, Paul?" I shook him. To think I'd trusted him. Surprisingly, he was still conscious, breathing shallow, but he still tried to talk.

"Explosion . . . grenade." Blue and green veins pressed against the skin of his face, blood trickled from his mouth. "Tra…tra…"

"Take your time, Paul." I tried to calm him down and rubbed his shoulder.

"Tra…trans..port." His adam's apple bobbed as he swallowed. "Jer…ri…cho."

"Transport?" Paul's body gave a final shudder. I turned toward Axel in confusion. "What's he talking about?"

I tried to ignore the tears burning my eyes. Axel wrapped his arms around me and held tight as I sniffed and took a few minutes to get myself together.

"Come on," He pulled me to my feet. "We need to get out of here."

I took a deep breath and straightened my shoulders. "What do we do now?"

Axel led me away from Paul's body. "He's back in Hell now. We get the book, learn how to use your power and destroy Randall. We won't let him win."

Unholy

Acknowledgements

I would like to thank my cousin for being my voice of reason and my biggest inspiration to finish this book. Thank you for being with me every step of the way on top of your already hectic life. None of this would have been possible if you had not voluntarily involved yourself in my novice attempt at expressing myself.

To all my family and friends who pestered me about when the book would be done, I'm so glad for your interest. Thank you sincerely. I am truly humbled by this experience. I never knew what hard work and persistence meant until I decided to try this creative outlet and I'm so proud of what I accomplished.

About K.S. Garner

I'm a young aspiring author. My ideas center around fantasy, YA and dystopian. FYI, I'm the laziest Hufflepuff you've ever met who believes doing dishes is an unfair chore best left for the elves at night. This is still a learning process for me but I'd love to hear from readers.

Email: ksgarnerauthor@gmail.com

Made in the USA
Monee, IL
20 November 2021

82372199R00100